I0563415

Cruel Obsession

The Billionaires' Club: Book 2

AE Moran

The Invisible Publishing Company

The Billionaires' Club Series

Contents

Chapter 1: Judah

I flick an invisible speck of lint off the seat of my limo and look out the window for the thousandth time. Then I check my phone.

I can't appreciate the immaculate seats or the neighborhood full of mansions outside.

The streetlights gleam through sweeping oak trees lining broad, curving avenues. Brick walls surround every house with ornate wrought-iron security gates across every driveway.

Some of these houses even have armed security personnel patrolling the grounds or standing guard at the driveway entrances.

I know everyone who lives on this street, but they don't see me sitting in the back of my limo. I look down at my phone again. It's ten-thirty-seven at night.

I'm the only person in the neighborhood who isn't in his house getting ready to go to sleep for the night.

I glance through the window again. Everything sounds quiet out there—or it appears to be. I look around at the limo's interior. It's a very nice limo—as if I haven't seen it often enough. I ride in it every d ay.

Just at that moment, my phone buzzes. I've been looking at it non-stop for three hours, but I was too busy thinking about the limo. I jump in surprise and look down at the screen.

A single word pops up in a text. *Now.*

I throw open the rear passenger door, slam it behind me, and stick my phone in my jacket pocket. Adrenaline pumps through my veins as I stride up the sidewalk, turn the corner, and enter the driveway of one of the houses.

The security guard at the entrance gate dips his chin at me. "Good evening, Mr. Hayes."

I only nod at him and keep on walking. I'm on a mission here.

I walk up to the house. It's a big mansion built of brown granite with mitered windows in the roof gables. Ten bedrooms occupy three different wings with an equestrian ring in the back, sprawling Victorian-style grounds, and the estate's own small forest lot.

None of that concerns me right now. This is deadly serious business.

I find the front door locked, so I unlock it with my own key. This is my house.

I turn off through the entrance foyer and charge up the stairs three at a time.

I make it halfway there before I hear screaming. The voice drifts down the hall from one of the side wings, floats onto the landing, and gets louder the higher I climb.

That sound cuts off when I get to the landing and then deep moans take its place. These aren't as loud, but they twist in my guts just as much. I know that sound.

I turn off into a bedroom and look down at my wife Skyla stark naked on all fours on the bed. Some jackass I've never seen before kneels behind her driving his prick into her from behind like the bitch she is.

She arches her hips into his thrusts and moans in deep satisfaction. I know that moan. She's definitely enjoying herself. She has her eyes closed so she doesn't see me at first.

At least she had the decency to do it in a guest room in another wing on the opposite end of the house.

She didn't do it in the bedroom we share, but that only pisses me off even more. She tried to hide it—as if she could get away with this somehow.

Her blonde curls sway with each thrust. They bounce against her cheeks and spill over her closed eyes.

I don't have to see her eyes to remember how those crystal blue pools used to glaze over for me.

How many other guys have they been glazing over for these past few months? Probably more than I can count.

Her full, ivory breasts bump each time he bangs into her from behind. Her perfect rose-petal nipples stand out hard and tight in her excitement.

He snarls down at her with his lip curled back from his teeth. He pants in time to his thrusts—until he sees me.

His face goes slack and the color drains from his cheeks, but his body keeps going. He must be so disconnected from his brain that he doesn't think fast enough.

My last shred of patience snaps. I didn't know before what I would do if and when I actually saw this for myself.

Maybe some fogged part of my brain still believed right up until this moment that this would all turn out to be some colossal misunderstanding.

Maybe I thought I would find out I made a mistake and she really was the most loyal wife I could hope for. No such luck.

I lunge into the room, seize the guy by the back of the neck, and rip him off the bed.

He struggles—as if he could overpower me. "Hey!" he yells and tries to turn back.

My wife's eyes pop open when she feels him slide out of her. That's when she sees me.

She stares at me with her mouth open. She's so sex-drunk that she doesn't react fast enough, either.

She starts to turn around. "Judah....!" she blurts out, but I'm already dragging the chump out of the room.

I shove him down the hall to the landing and then down the stairs. He tries to turn around in my grip. "At least let me put my clothes on first...."

I grit my teeth to stop myself from saying anything. I wouldn't be able to come up with anything to say to this piece of shit anyway.

He stumbles on the stairs. I shake him by the neck to make him stand up straight.

I get halfway down to the foyer before my wife catches up with me. "You don't understand, Judah!" she stammers. "I can explain everything. We can work this out. Let him go, Judah! We can discuss this like rational adults. There's no need to get violent."

I snarl over my shoulder through gritted teeth. "Oh, there's plenty of need to get violent."

"You can't do this, Judah!" she hollers.

I don't answer her at all. I can definitely do this. I can do this and so much more.

I get as far as the front door, yank it open, and march the asshole outside. He's still stark naked.

Four security guards meet us on the steps outside. I give the guy a hard shove and send him staggering into the security guards' waiting arms. "Get him the hell out of here."

Then I turn to my wife.

She shrinks away from the open door so the security guys won't see her naked. Don't ask me why she cares about that when she's sleeping with half the county.

She actually had the presence of mind to bring some of her clothes downstairs. She clutches them against her chest, but they don't hide anything. What a whore she is.

I grab her by the back of the neck and start marching her toward the open front door, too.

She screams and tries to struggle, but she isn't strong enough to break my grip. She's even less capable of putting up a fight than her boyfriend—or whatever the hell he is.

"Judah!" she shrieks. "You can't do this to me! I have rights! You can't throw me out of my own house!"

"This is my house, you bitch!" I snarl down at her and snatch the clothes out of her hands. "I paid for these! They're mine—not yours! Everything you own is mine."

"YOU CAN'T DO THIS, JUDAH!!" she screeches. "LET ME GO!"

"Nope," I mutter and yank her toward the door.

The security guys stand around outside ready to take her off my hands, but I'm not playing that. She deserves so much worse than the guy.

I drag her outside. The security guards separate to let me through and then follow on both sides while I drag her stumbling and screaming to the gate. It's still open.

The private investigator I hired to track her stands off to one side watching. We've been planning this for weeks.

The guard at the gate stands on the other side. All of them watch me haul this piece of trash out to the curb.

I have to stop myself from throwing her on the ground. I want to, but that would be too much. This is enough.

I push her away and send her stumbling into the street stark naked where she belongs.

"Get the hell off my property and don't ever come back!" I bark. "Don't ever set foot on my property again unless you want to get arrested."

She trips and staggers a few steps before she turns around. She doesn't have a stitch on. I don't even care that all these guys get to see her as naked as the day she was born.

She might have been backing it up to any of them for all I know. She could have been doing my whole security team.

She rushes back toward the gate trying to get inside, but all the security guys close in front of me to block her. They line up in a barricade so she can't get through.

I back away and the guard shuts the gate with me inside. All the rest of them stay out there to make sure the skank doesn't come back onto the grounds.

"JUDAH!!!" she bellows after me. "YOU CAN'T DO THIS TO ME!! YOU CAN'T JUST THROW ME OUT!! I HAVE RIGHTS!! THIS IS MY HOUSE AS MUCH AS YOURS!! YOU WON'T GET AWAY WITH THIS!! JUDAH!!!"

I turn away and walk back to the house. Her voice echoes through the neighborhood. Lights come on in windows on either side and down the street. Now everyone will look outside and see her naked on the street in the middle of the night. Good.

I shut the door and block out the noise. Now I'm alone in this house, but I know exactly what I have to do. She thinks this is her house as much as mine.

I have to act fast to stop her from taking anything of mine. I have to make sure she stays gone and doesn't come back to haunt me.

Chapter 2: Piper

I try to pay attention to the legal brief on my computer screen, but I can't help checking the time. I still have ten minutes before my appointment with Judah Hayes.

I need to concentrate, but my nerves get the better of me. Judah's reputation is only half as impressive as Judah himself.

He's one of the richest men in New York and also one with the most impressive presence. He's tall, powerful, serious, and always, always on his game.

He's also very married—so why is he coming to see me—a divorce lawyer? This can't be anything good.

I try one last time to shake those thoughts out of my head and focus on the work in front of me, but just then, my phone buzzes on the desk in front of me.

A text comes through from the receptionist out front. *Judah Hayes is here early. He's sitting in the waiting room.*

I snatch my phone and text back with trembling fingers. *Send him in now. Don't keep him waiting.*

I close the brief file and stand up. I go through a flurry of confused, hopeless movements trying to decide how to get ready to meet Judah. This isn't how I planned to meet him, but okay. It looks like we're doing this.

I walk around my desk and get to the door just as he walks in. I smile up at him. He's even taller in person than he looks in pictures.

He shaves his hair close enough to his scalp to show the deep, chocolate-brown skin underneath. His square jaw, prominent cheekbones, and strong eyebrow ridges form a chiseled, classic look like a statue of some African god carved out of marble.

I hold out my hand. "Thank you for coming in, Mr. Hayes. I'm Piper Lagrange. Please—take a seat."

"Thank you for seeing me on such short notice." He moves into my office, but he doesn't sit down. He stands there waiting for me to walk around my desk to my own chair.

He wears a perfectly tailored blue suit. His stark white shirt collar and shirt cuffs somehow looks even more striking against his dark neck and hands. I can't remember seeing any man look so good in a suit.

I step in front of my chair to sit down.....and right at that moment, his deep brown eyes dip to my body. It's an appraising look, but also the appreciative look of a man checking out a woman he finds attractive.

I don't consider myself attractive. I think of myself as blocky and utilitarian, especially when I'm wearing a business suit.

My suit might be perfectly tailored and top-of-the-line expensive, but it's nothing to write home about. It also doesn't do my body any favors. It's just a business suit like every other.

Judah doesn't seem to think so, though. His eyes linger on the neckline of my blouse with three buttons open. I know he can't see my cleavage, but he might as well be looking straight through my clothes at my bra underneath.

Then his eyes migrate farther south, over my blazer buttoned close to my waist, and down to my hips where my tight pencil skirt covers my legs to my knees.

I squirm when I feel him undressing me with his eyes, but the whole thing happens in a split second before I sit down in my chair. Now I'm facing him across my desk. He has nothing to look at but my face.

Even then, his eyes take in every detail of my straight brown hair hanging past my shoulders, my understated gold necklace and earrings, and my simple, tasteful makeup.

Plenty of people tell me I'm pretty, but I never believed them. I look like every other businesswoman on the planet.

I fold my hands on the desk, but they give Judah plenty to look at, too. He sees my nails and the gold chain bracelet around my wrist. Does it mean anything to him? He must see businesswomen like me every day of the week.

I clear my throat. I'm working here. I'm not on display. "So what can I do for you, Mr. Hayes?" I ask—like I don't already know.

"I want to get a divorce—obviously." He barely smiles. "I mean, I'm getting a divorce one way or the other. Wilson Avery recommended you, so I need someone to represent me."

I pretend to raise my eyebrows like I didn't know that's why he came. He wouldn't come to see a divorce lawyer if he wasn't getting a divorce.

"So what are the grounds for the divorce?" I ask.

"Infidelity—on her part. I hired a private investigator to track her down, so we have a ton of evidence that she was cheating for months. Then we set her up so I could walk in on her doing it with a guy in my house. I threw her out—and him out. You could say I humiliated her. I threw her out stark naked on the street with nothing in the middle of the night and I told her never to set foot on my property again."

Now I really do raise my eyebrows. "Wow. Brutal."

A very slight smile twitches his lips and he immediately wipes it away. He goes back to being carved out of ice. "She deserved it."

"So what kind of settlement are you hoping to get out of this?"

"No settlement. She gets nothing. That's the only outcome I'll accept."

I have to stop myself from arguing with him. He's too determined. Everybody knows it. I would never be able to talk him out of this.

"Listen, Mr. Hayes," I tell him. "You're obviously still angry over your wife's infidelity. You want to punish her by cutting her off with nothing. I understand that. Unfortunately, the law doesn't work that way. Depending on the stipulations of your marriage...."

"We have a pre-nup," he interrupts. "The pre-nup specifically states that she gets no settlement in the case of infidelity—and I have all my assets protected in trusts and corporations. She wouldn't be able to get anything out of me even without the pre-nup."

"I'll need to see all the documentation—on all your assets."

He stiffens in his chair and the tension in the room spikes. A guy as powerful as Judah Hayes won't want some stranger going through his affairs. I have to tread carefully here.

"I'll need to see all the evidence you have of her infidelity, all the records of both of your spending habits—everything," I tell him. "This will be the best way to protect you."

He actually shifts in his chair and looks away. "I guess I expected that."

"If you've protected yourself as well as you say you have, then you shouldn't have anything to worry about."

He lowers his voice to a deadly growl. "I better not."

"Just send me everything you have and let me take a look. Then I'll be able to advise you better." I open my mouth to ask something else and hesitate.

"What?" he asks. "What's wrong?"

I try to wave it away, but I have to ask. "So.....you own......twenty companies—all under the North Star Investments parent corporation? Am I right? I think I heard that, but it was a few years ago."

"Twenty-five, but they're all public corporate structures. She wouldn't be able to do anything to them. It's my shares in those companies she would probably try to get. They're owned in my name—or they were."

"What do you mean, they were?"

"I put them in trust. I told her I wanted to put everything in a family trust for our children—if we had them—or my children—whatever. I told her my wealth would be better protected that way and she agreed."

"So.....what assets do you own that aren't protected? What about your house?"

"That's in the trust, too."

"Do you own any assets that aren't protected by a trust?"

"No," he replies. "The only things I own that aren't protected by trusts are my clothes, a few electronic devices, some sports gear, and maybe my personal effects like my toothbrush and stuff like that."

I burst out laughing before I think to stop myself. I can't imagine him doing anything as mundane as brushing his teeth. He's so far removed from all those human concerns.

He obviously does brush his teeth, though. He takes impeccable care of himself.

He proves it by biting back another grin. I catch a fleeting glimpse of strong, white, sharp teeth in his mouth.

"I do brush my teeth, Ms. Lagrange," he tells me.

"I'm sure you do." I pull myself together. "Well, I have to say you are probably the best protected client I've ever had. If you're right, then this should be an open and shut case. I don't see how she can get any of your wealth or assets."

He goes deadly serious again and his eyes slice away. "I'm sure she can find a way."

"What makes you say that?"

"Because she's conniving and manipulative."

"How conniving and manipulative are we talking about? Has she ever done anything you might think of as dangerous?"

"No, nothing like that, but she lied to my face for years before we got married. She might have been screwing half the Eastern Seaboard even then. When I threw her out, she started raving about how the house was as much hers as it is mine and then she said I wouldn't get away with this."

"Ah." I nod. "I see."

"I don't care what it takes. She isn't getting a penny from me."

"I understand, but I won't know where I stand until I see the documentation. Have you actually filed for divorce yet?"

"Yes. I did it yesterday."

"How did you pay for the private investigator?" I ask. "You must have a bank account you use for personal expenses."

"Yes, I do, but I keep the balance at a minimum. I got in the habit of saving when I was younger, so my corporate salary goes straight into investments. The returns from those investments get reinvested."

"Then where do your personal expense funds come from? I apologize for prying, but I need to know every detail of your financial position so I can pursue this case with the best strategy to protect your interests."

"That's all right. I don't mind talking about it. I have one investment that pays into my personal daily operating account."

"Which investment is it?" I ask. "Is it protected by the trust, too?"

"Yes, the trust owns the stock, but the dividend goes into my account."

"Do you get a beneficiary distribution from the trust?"

"I'm not a beneficiary of the trust."

My head shoots up. "You aren't? Why not?"

"It's a family trust like I told you. I set it up for any children I might have in the future. They're the only beneficiaries of the trust."

"But.....you don't have any children....do you?" I squirm in my seat. "I didn't think you did."

"I don't—not yet. The trust is set up to benefit any direct blood descendants I have no matter who they are. I'm not a beneficiary and neither is Skyla. All the returns from all my investments get reinvested until my children reach maturity—and even then, there are conditions the beneficiaries have to meet before they access the money or even receive a distribution."

I raise my eyebrows. "That's interesting. I've never heard of anything like that before."

"I don't see why it's so surprising. How else am I supposed to preserve my wealth for my children and grandchildren?"

"It's impressive that you thought of this before you got married. Not many people think to take these precautions beforehand. It makes me wonder if you had some notion that your soon-to-be-ex-wife might not have been as upright as you thought."

"I set up the trust before I met her. I dated a few people before I married her. I was already doing pretty well for myself and my money brought the gold diggers out of the woodwork. That's when I realized I needed to take steps to make sure none of them got their grubby little fingers on anything of mine."

"Wow," I remark, "I don't think I've ever met a client as insightful and well-prepared. It shows amazing foresight and presence of mind. Most people let their feelings dictate their actions."

"That isn't me," he replies.

I find myself measuring him. "I see that. Well, send me the documentation and we can get started."

He pulls out his phone. "Do I need to stick around while you go over everything?"

"It will take me days to go through everything. I'll call you if we need to review anything."

"I can have my accountant come over and explain things if you need him to."

I smile at him, but he doesn't see me while he's tapping on his phone. "I think I can handle it. I've seen accounts, trusts, and corporate structural instruments before."

His eyes shoot up to meet mine and he immediately looks away. "I'm sorry. I shouldn't have implied that. I'm not used to dealing with people who know my business as well as I do." He puts his phone away. "You should have the paperwork by now."

"Thank you. I feel confident we can bring this to a conclusion that satisfies you."

"The only conclusion that will satisfy me is if she walks away with nothing. If I find out she has anything I paid for, I want it back."

"Can you think of anything that would be? Can you think of anything she might have that you paid for that we haven't covered?"

"I don't think so. I've thought about nothing else since I found out she was cheating. I tried to make sure she didn't have anything I paid for—but it's a little hard because I paid for everything since the day we met. I like to be generous when I date."

I can't help smiling at him. So big, bad, scary Judah Hayes has a soft side after all. "What did you buy her? Did you buy her jewelry and diamonds and expensive shoes and purses and stuff like that?"

"No, she said she didn't care about that—but she obviously did. She made a big deal when we first dated that she didn't care about my money—which was obviously another lie."

"So what do you mean when you say you paid for everything?"

"I helped her with her bills, paid her rent, got her car fixed—stuff like that."

"But you bought her clothes and shoes and purses after you married her—right?"

"Yes, but only then. Up until we actually got married, she said she wanted to take care of herself even though she obviously couldn't."

"So.....you never bought her gifts?"

"Only for birthdays, anniversaries, Christmas—stuff like that."

"You understand you can't get those things back, right?" I ask. "She gets to keep gifts."

He shrugs. "Whatever."

"So what gifts did you buy her for birthdays, anniversaries, Christmas, and stuff like that? What did she like?"

"Stuffed animals."

My head whips around again. "Excuse me?"

"She collects stuffed animals—and everything Pikachu. She's a Pikachu fanatic, so anything Pikachu."

I blink at him for a second and then do my best not to snort with laughter. It comes out anyway.

He bites back another grin. "Laugh all you want."

I finally let it out. "So is her collection at your house?"

"No, I packed it up the next day and sent all the boxes to her mother's house in the Bronx. Skyla had a massive collection already before I met her and she moved it all into our bedroom at my house. I never liked it. It creeped me out to try to sleep in the same room with all those stuffed animals staring at me, so I got rid of everything right away—that same night."

I bust out laughing again. I can't help it. I fall over my desk and bury my head in my arms before I straighten up and try unsuccessfully to pull myself together. "Sorry!" I gasp. "I know I shouldn't laugh about this."

He tries to stay serious, but he has to work hard not to smile. "That's okay. I know it's ridiculous."

I wave my hand in front of my face and have to get myself a tissue to wipe the tears of laughter out of my eyes. "I'm sorry. I don't mean to make light of your situation. I guess there's nothing left to do but for me to look at the documentation. We can go from there. I'm sure Skyla will let us know if you have anything she wants."

His expression turns to ice. "I'm sure she will."

I stand up and hold out my hand. "It was a pleasure meeting you. I look forward to working with you."

He stands up and shakes my hand. "Likewise. Thank you for taking this on."

I have to remark again how tall and powerfully built he is. He makes me feel tiny by comparison.

He leaves and I sit down in my desk chair. As soon as the door shuts, I break down laughing again. I can't stop thinking about Judah trying to sleep in a room surrounded by a million Chucky-style psycho stuffed animals.

I really need to get serious about this case, so I turn to the documentation he sent me. The first file is a bunch of corporate instruments for all his companies.

The guy is loaded to the eyeballs with money and investments, but he's right. Everything is secured in trusts or covered by the articles of incorporation for one enterprise or another.

I go over his family trust, but that looks solid, too. The pre-nup is standard with no surprises. From what I can tell, Judah really is as protected as he says. The guy covers his bases. I'll give him that much.

The only question is how a guy as astute as this let such a floozy end-run him into this marriage. Maybe he wanted to believe her lies about not wanting his money.

If he had bad experiences with gold diggers before he met Skyla, he might have been extra sensitive and easily swayed by someone who pretended not to be one. I guess I can't blame him for that.

I unzip the folder from the private investigator. The most recent file is a collection of video clips from security cameras all over Judah Hayes's house.

The first clip shows some guy banging Skyla Hayes in a big fancy bedroom, but I don't see any stuffed animals. This must be a guest room or something.

I find myself snickering at the thought. Maybe she didn't want to corrupt her precious stuffed companions by letting them see some bozo drill her like the street tramp she obviously is.

The same clip shows Judah storming in, grabbing the guy, and dragging him stark naked out of the house. One of the camera angles shows a glimpse of Judah's expression.

He locks his jaw in a solid block of granite. His eyes narrow and flash with fury. Dang. I better never do anything to make that guy mad.

He hauls the offender outside and then another clip shows Judah handing the guy over to the security team. They take the guy off somewhere out of sight.

The next series of clips shows what Judah did to Skyla. She's buck-naked through the entire process. He throws her out on the street in the middle of the night without a stitch on. His retribution is every bit as brutal as I said if not more so.

The rest of the folder contains more footage of Skyla getting nailed by a bunch of different guys in a bunch of different locations.

Some of the footage has obviously been shot with a telescopic lens from another car. This footage shows her getting railed in the backs of cars, in alleys, in restaurant bathrooms, and in the bedrooms of other houses. She sure kept busy while he was out there conquering the world.

I cringe when I remember how serious Judah acted just now. No wonder he's pissed about this. No wonder he wants to cut her off with nothing. She humiliated him.

Chapter 3: Judah

I walk into The Billionaires' Club and head for the pool table. Lane Prince, Jackson Metcalf, and Kevin Drake stand over there.

I sense an instant change when I cross the room. No one stops what they're doing or changes their tone at all. Maybe the change is me.

My wife cheated on me. The story broke all over the news this week, so everyone knows the details.

I would have liked to post the video footage on the internet so everyone knows what a tramp she is. It would serve her right.

I can't even do that. The world finding out what a tramp she is only makes me look bad.

I would pay a lot of money to stop everyone from finding out I'm divorcing her for infidelity. I can't stop everyone from finding out, though. It's in the divorce filing so it's public record.

Jackson shakes my hand when I join their circle. "How you doing, man? How's the cage match shaping up?"

I only nod. I appreciate my friends' support, but I can't enjoy their sense of humor—not today. "It's looking pretty good."

"I hear you engaged Piper Lagrange," Lane adds. "She's supposed to be the best. She got Wilson Avery a great settlement."

"She's going over all the documentation now," I reply. "She says she's confident she can bring it to a satisfactory conclusion."

"It sucks about the publicity, though," Kevin chimes in. "No one likes having their personal business dragged through the streets."

"I don't care about that as long as the bitch doesn't get anything."

"Are you sure you want to do that?" Kevin asks. "Maybe you should just pay her off so she shuts up and disappears."

"I'll never pay her off." I hear myself acting too harshly, but it comes out anyway. "I don't give a damn what the public thinks as long as she goes right back to the gutter where she belongs."

"You might have to care," Lane points out. "You run investment firms. If you bring bad publicity to your companies, your customers might decide not to invest with you."

I open my mouth to tell him I don't give a crap about that, either, but right then, Giovanni Nowaczyk bursts out laughing across the room.

I wouldn't normally pay any attention to that, but the sound grates on my nerves. I jerk upright to glare at him, but he doesn't even look at me.

He's in the middle of talking to Rory Kahn and Niko Holloway. They're all younger than me and the men in my circle. Rory, Niko, and Giovanni could be talking about anything. They aren't necessarily laughing at me.

They better not be, but the sound of that laughter grates my nerves on end. I need to get out of here.

I wait for a break in the conversation and make an excuse to leave. How did Skyla ruin this for me along with everything else? I can't even enjoy my time at The Billionaires' Club without worrying about this.

My driver meets me downstairs with my limo and drives me back to my house. I go up to my room and look around. It looks a whole lot different without Skyla's stuffed animal collection in here. The room looks more like a hotel room.

I sit down on the edge of the bed and look through the big bay windows at the grounds outside. The New York skyline pokes up above the trees.

This house sounds way too quiet, now that I'm the only person living here. Skyla didn't spend that much time here before I threw her out. Now she's gone completely.

I don't want her back, but I don't like my life when I'm alone. I want someone. I just don't know who.

Every one of these setbacks makes me more guarded and mistrustful. This divorce is going to make me even more of a magnet for women who only want my money and the luxury lifestyle I can provide for them.

Forget dating apps or matchmaking services or anything like that. How would I even meet anyone?

Everyone I know is either an employee in one of my companies or I already work with them in some other business capacity. They're off the table for me.

I can't stay here thinking about it, so I tell my driver to take me downtown. I don't know what to do. I'm single for the first time in years. I'm at loose ends with nowhere to go and nothing to do.

I decide to take a walk through Central Park. I really should take some security with me. The sun is going down, but I need to be alone right now.

I head for the corner, but before I can enter the park, I run into Saul Gottlieb and his son Asher. "Come join us for a drink," Saul tells me. "The night is young. You don't want to go in there."

I actually don't not with the shadows starting to lengthen. I take Saul up on his offer and we cross the street to an Irish style pub.

It's a lot busier than I expect. I thought I'd be sitting in a quiet place having a drink with Saul and Asher.

People crowd the bar and more stand around between the tables that are already loaded with more patrons. Saul, Asher, and I get separated the minute we walk in the door.

Four guys sit in chairs at the other end of the room playing Irish music on fiddles, guitars, and flutes. I don't see what everyone is celebrating, but everyone seems to be enjoying themselves.

At least I don't have to think about my divorce here. No one here knows me apart from Saul and Asher. I can't even see them in the crowd. They might not be in the same room anymore.

The music sounds cheerful and the atmosphere lightens my mood. Maybe I needed this more than I realized.

I elbow my way to the bar. I'm the only black person here, but no one seems to care. No one notices me at all even though I'm bigger than everyone else, too.

I finally force myself to the bar and order a glass of pineapple juice. I don't drink, but sipping a nice glass of something seems to fit with this occasion.

I'm going through a divorce. I guess I can relax for once just because.

I take a sip and turn around to scan the room. That's when I see Piper Lagrange standing at the other end of the bar. She's talking to three other guys in business suits. I don't recognize them.

She's much shorter than they are. She can't be more than five-foot-six with a petite figure, but she's stunning in an understated way.

She wears her hair combed straight down to her shoulders with very simple makeup and jewelry. She's one of the few women I've seen in the business world who doesn't try to go over the top to impress everyone with her appearance.

She can't hide her pure beauty, though. She doesn't have Skyla's drop-dead hourglass figure, knockout chest, or J-Lo booty. Piper doesn't need them.

Her body has a tight, compact look that is all business. She wears her suits cut in a vintage style. They hug her waist much tighter and blend into her skirt. She doesn't wear the square, straight style blazer that looks like something a man might wear.

Her suit makes her slim body look every bit as delicious as a woman twice as curvy. Piper's simplicity and straightforward attitude make her appealing in a completely different way.

I want to talk to her, but she's too deep in conversation with the other three guys. I don't want to interrupt—and I don't want to talk about whatever they're talking about. I want to talk to her. If I went over there, I might wind up talking to the guys and I don't want that.

I settle down on my stool to watch her. She fascinates me in a way I can't understand.

She knows everything about me. She's seen the files from the private investigator, so she now knows more about me than almost anyone alive.

I shudder to think what conclusions she came to from seeing all that, but something tells me she doesn't judge me for it. She's the only person I know who gives me that impression.

I can't picture her holding it against me—as if she could hold it against me. I don't think she's laughing at me behind my back. I don't get the impression that she thinks less of me because my ex-wife is a shameless skank who spread her legs for half of Manhattan.

That's the problem, I really don't know anything about Piper. I know her record. She's represented some of the richest men in New York through disastrous divorces much worse than mine.

They all wound up settling, though, and I don't plan to settle.

She seemed to accept my decision on that. She didn't try to talk me out of it. That impresses me. She understands. Does she have some cheating ex in her past?

Don't ask me why I'm getting so interested in her because she's my lawyer. We have a business arrangement—nothing more. It could never be anything else.

She won't always be my lawyer, though. I'll get divorced and then Piper will stop being my lawyer. Something might happen then.

I don't want to wait until then, and right at that moment, the three guys she's talking to walk away. They leave her alone at the bar and she turns back to give the bartender a tip. Now's my chance.

Chapter 4: Piper

I snap my wallet shut and put it in my purse. I'm just about to hang it over my shoulder and leave the bar when Judah Hayes comes up to me. "Hello," he greets me. "Do you come here often?"

I make a face. "Funny. I'm gonna go out on a limb and say *you* don't come here often."

"I've never been here before in my life...but I like it." He looks around at the other patrons and the band in the corner.

He looks a lot more relaxed here than he did at my office. He actually looks kind of happy—if he's even capable of that.

"You like it?" I repeat. "Why do you like it? This isn't exactly your scene, is it?"

"No, it isn't. Maybe that's why I like it—because it's so completely different from anything I'm used to. Maybe that's why it feels like a relief to come in here. I can hide from reality. No one knows me. I can be anonymous here."

I look up at him. He stands at least six inches taller than me. His dark skin stands out even more around all these white people, but he never looked more magnetic.

His eyes glisten with something like excitement. He smiles easily. I never thought I'd ever see that.

"So what are you doing here?" he asks and looks around again. "Are you with someone here?"

"No, I'm not with anyone here. I had to meet some former clients about a case I did for them. They wanted to discuss some of the details. They were the ones who chose to meet here."

"It isn't the most obvious place for a business meeting, is it?" he asks and then levels me with a stare that cuts right to the marrow of my bones. "Are you seeing anyone?"

"You just engaged me to represent you in a divorce. You shouldn't be asking me that."

"I'm not asking you out. I'm just asking if you're seeing anyone."

I look away. "No, I'm not seeing anyone."

"Why not?" he asks. "Why don't you at least have a boyfriend or something?"

"Because I'm not good-looking enough to have a boyfriend—or anything else. No guys want me when they can get someone so much better looking."

He stares at me with that brutal intensity he used in my office. His eyes have a way of unpeeling every defense—and it isn't just me.

I've seen pictures and interviews of him doing it to everyone. He looks straight through the person he's talking to.

Then my heart stops when he drags his gaze down my body. He scrutinizes every inch and curve exactly the way he did in my office. He unpeels that, too, and undresses me right there in the middle of the bar.

"You're definitely good-looking enough," he murmurs under his breath.

That voice caresses me all over. I shiver as the low, husky sensation of his voice slithers between my legs and up my thighs to my panties. I can just feel him stroking me there with that hypnotic voice.

I gulp and force myself to look away. I'm not thinking that about a man I just took as a client.

I try to brush it off by dismissing the question. "It doesn't matter because I'm not seeing anyone and I'm not going to be seeing anyone. I have too much work to do as it is."

"Have a drink with me."

My head shoots up so fast I make myself dizzy. "Are you crazy? I can't have a drink with you!"

"Why not?" He nods at the stool next to me. "Sit down. What are you drinking?"

"I can't have a drink with you because I'm your lawyer and you're my client."

"We can have a drink as lawyer and client, then." He waves the bartender over and asks the guy what I'm having. Judah orders another one for me even though I still haven't agreed to have a drink with him.

"You really shouldn't be doing this," I tell him.

"Doing what? I'm just sitting here drinking my drink. I'm not doing anything."

"You're in the middle of a disastrous divorce after getting cheated on for months. You aren't in any condition to have a drink with anyone—especially not someone you think is good-looking enough to have a boyfriend."

He laughs. This is the first time I've seen him laugh. His whole face lights up and his brilliant, strong white teeth show between his dark brown lips.

He has a sparkling, boyish laugh that somehow makes his features look even more antique and godlike.

He turns those twinkling eyes on me—and now I know without a shred of doubt that he isn't asking me to have a drink as lawyer and client. He's asking me in that way—like he wants to ask me out—except that we're already out.

He dips his eyes to the stool again. "Sit down. Nothing is going to happen—not with all these people around. We're just two business associates having a drink because we happened to bump into each other at a bar. That's all."

He says it, but I already know that isn't true. This is much more than that.

Every minute I spend in his presence confirms it. Every flick of his eyes over my suit and body and neck and mouth feels like he's already touching me.....fingering me.....grasping me.....licking me.....

I swallow hard. I really need to walk away right now. I should tell him I can't represent him, but I've already started working on the case.

If he went to some other lawyer, he would have to show them the folder of video files. He would have to confide all his business and personal secrets to some stranger.

Thinking that makes up my mind for me. I don't want him to go to someone else. I don't want anyone else to represent him.

I want to make sure his ex gets what she deserves. I don't want another lawyer to tell Judah to settle the divorce and move on. He deserves that vindication if nothing else.

He doesn't act like the infidelity bothers him—at least, he doesn't act like it here. He showed it more in my office.

Of course it bothers him. It must. No one could watch their spouse screw around with so many people in so many different locations for so long without it bothering them.

He's strong. He hides it, but it must really eat away at him on the inside. That's why he doesn't want her to get anything from him. She's already taken too much.

I sit down on the stool and the bartender brings my drink and another glass of juice for Judah. I can't look at him. I can't let myself see how satisfied he is that I'm sitting here having a drink with him.

"So tell me what you think of the files I sent you."

I don't look up. "The video footage was pretty bad—much worse than I thought."

"Do you think the court will frown on me throwing her out the way I did?"

I shrug. "I guess not."

"Do you think I did the wrong thing by throwing her out the way I did?"

My head spins around before I think to stop myself. "Why do you care whether I think you did the wrong thing? You already did it. You can't go back and change it."

He faces front and stares into his beer. "I guess I just doubt myself."

"You—doubt yourself? I find that hard to believe."

He glances at me and I realize I'm sitting way too close to him. His body radiates power and unstoppable, irresistible attraction from inches away.

I get another blast of his body luring me in with its magnetic pull. He would touch me right now if he thought he could get away with it. He would do a lot more than touch me.

For some reason, the fact that he holds himself back in public makes him even more intoxicatingly attractive. He doesn't touch me because doing so would be completely out of line.

He wants to, though. He makes no effort at all to hide that. He throbs with it under his suit. I've never felt this from anyone.

His body, face, and eyes vibrate with smoldering intensity like an animal stalking its prey. He only has to glance at me to make me tremble.

"I guess I've always prided myself on keeping my composure in all situations," he goes on. "I don't like that I lost it with her—even then."

"But you didn't lose your composure. You didn't react violently. You threw them both out of your house—which I guess you had every right to do. I checked the documentation. The house is owned by your family trust with you as the trustee. The trust gives you the legal right to live in the house and manage its upkeep and security at your discretion. That would give you the right to decide who to allow on the premises. The pre-nup specifically states that infidelity is grounds for immediate and unequivocal divorce without recourse, settlement, or compensation. So we could argue that the marriage officially ended the very first time she cheated on you. So by that logic, she was trespassing by bringing whoever he was onto the premises and doing it with him there—which means you had the legal right to throw her out."

I force myself to stop talking. I'm rambling about a bunch of legal gibberish he doesn't care about.

I take a drink just to put something in my mouth to stop myself from saying anything else.

"Thank you for saying that," he murmurs. "It means a lot."

"Sorry," I mutter. "I was planning on telling you all that at our first meeting. I guess I just don't seem to be able to shut up when it comes to anything legal."

He smiles at me. "I appreciate you saying it. It's nothing I haven't thought of, but it helps to hear someone else say it—someone with some legal expertise."

"I don't know why you doubt yourself. You obviously have plenty of grounds to divorce her."

His eyes glitter with an extra dimension of depth. "Do you have something like this in your past? Is this what makes you so passionate about it?"

I can't look at him. "Nothing like this—but yeah, I guess you could say I went through something similar. It was no picnic."

Out of nowhere, his big, strong, muscular hand falls on my shoulder. He squeezes. "We can commiserate together. At least I'm not the only one. I felt pretty stupid when I found out how bad it was."

I barely choke out, "You aren't stupid."

He takes his hand off my shoulder, but that one powerful squeeze sends shockwaves through me. I should run from him, but I can't.

I want to throw myself at him—or have him throw himself at me.

He needs someone. He's probably in the breakup stage where he wants someone to fill his wife's place. He's suffering from that loss.

I can't be that person, but I want to give him that. I want to make him feel better.

This goes way beyond that, though. He's too big, too powerful, and too self-possessed to lean on a woman for emotional support—not in that way.

He would be predatory in bed—but not in a creepy, dangerous way. He would be just as commanding and determined in bed as he is in every other area of his life. He isn't capable of anything else.

Going there with him would NOT be about making him feel better. He wouldn't let it.

He would take over. He would conquer. He would dominate just like he dominates in business.

It doesn't matter because I'm not going there with him. I'm going to finish my drink and go home. That's all. Nothing else.

He snaps me back to reality. "So what about the rest of it? If you were going to talk to me about it in a meeting, why not talk to me about it now? Does the trust look as solid as I hope it does?"

I nod. "It looks that way on the surface. Everything you put into the trust before you met her should be safe. She might try to claim any earnings or assets you acquired while you were together."

His features harden. "Hell no. She is NOT getting her hands on those, either."

"You don't want her to, but the court might not see it the same way."

"How could she get her hands on them when she did nothing to earn them? If you're right about the infidelity ending the marriage, then her claim on my assets would have ended the minute she cheated, too."

I shrug. "We can try it, but it doesn't usually work out that way in court."

He scowls and all his cheery demeanor evaporates. He glares down at his glass.

Without thinking, I shoot out my hand and squeeze his arm. I shouldn't be drinking. It happens so fast that I don't think to stop myself.

I squeeze on his bicep. He feels just as strong, muscular, and taut under his jacket as he looks everywhere else.

"Try not to dwell on it," I tell him. "It won't do any good. Just try to go on with your life as best you can and put the pieces back together."

"That's what I am doing," he mutters under his breath.

I let go of his arm just as fast, but it's already too late. I touched him.

That squeeze is completely innocent, but it doesn't feel like it. I encouraged that body of his to vibrate to me the way it wants to. Does he feel the way I respond to his energy?

He looks over at me. His eyes make me weak in the knees even though I'm sitting down. "I appreciate you talking to me about this. I haven't been able to talk to anyone about it."

I gulp and try to turn away, but his eyes hold me captive. He gazes into my eyes like a lover—like we're already in bed together and he's seeing me laid bare for him to do with as he pleases.

God, am I really thinking that? Am I really thinking about lying in bed with him?

I have to get out of here before this turns into something I'll regret. I already regret it.

I down the rest of my drink. "I better go," I tell him. "I'll email you in a few days to arrange another meeting...."

I glance at him. I was about to say that our next meeting will be in my office where I can be certain we won't get distracted by any suggestive pretext.

I realize in that moment that I'll never be able to meet him anywhere, anytime, under any circumstances without some suggestive pretext. It will always be there simmering with buried tension.

"Thank you for talking, Piper," he murmurs again. "I really appreciate it."

I feel my cheeks flushing. "Anytime." Damn it! I shouldn't have said that.

"Is there anything I can do for you?" he asks. "Can I drive you anywhere.....?"

"No!" I blurt out way too loudly. "I'll be in touch soon. Then we can....." Come on, Piper. Try to make some sense here. "We can go over the details of your case and clarify a few things in the documentation." I shoot him as fake a smile as I can muster. "Try not to drink too much, okay? She isn't worth it."

He smiles back, but it's a big smile of genuine appreciation—or maybe it's something more. "Thank you. Your understanding means a lot."

I feel myself blushing. Just standing in front of him excites me. I need to get away from him so I can get myself under control.

Chapter 5: Piper

I race out of the bar to put as much distance between myself and Judah as I can. Sweet Jesus, what did I get myself into?

As soon as I stand up off the bar stool, I feel how wet my panties are. Walking makes it even more obvious.

The slippery wetness caresses my sensitive tissues when I walk. That sensation makes me feel hot and sexy. God, what is wrong with me?

I already know what's wrong with me. Judah is unbelievably hot—and not just his appearance. Just sitting on the bar stool next to him makes my blood race.

I wilt against the wall outside, shut my eyes, and try to catch my breath. I feel like I just made out with him in the bathroom stall or something, but I don't do that. His ex does that. I don't.

I can't stop shivering. I really need to stop thinking about Judah like this, but any thought about him sends me spiraling back there. God knows how many times I'll have to meet him before his divorce finally wraps up.

Will every meeting turn out like this one? I sure hope not.

Maybe things will be different when he comes to my office where we can talk to each other across my desk.

I don't see how that's possible. I'll be looking into his eyes head on. He'll be able to look at my body exactly the way he did last time. I won't be able to stop him.

Just knowing he'll look at me like that almost knocks me over. I reel off into another dizzy spell. The force of his presence overwhelms me even when I'm not near him.

This is bad. This is really bad. I have to do something about this. Just don't ask me what.

I push myself off the wall to approach the curb and hail a cab. Thank God I didn't drive anywhere with him. Who knows what would have happened then?

I turn around and stop dead in my tracks when I come face to face with Skyla—Skyla Hayes, Judah's wife. She isn't even his ex yet because the divorce is still pending.

She glares at me in venomous fury. I've never seen her like this before. I've only ever seen her smiling in angelic innocence in every other picture I've seen of her.

That isn't true. I've seen more than I ever wanted to see in the private investigator's zip folder. I've seen Skyla Hayes in every compromising position there is.

I've seen her straddling bathroom toilet seats getting her ass bumped into next week. I've seen her bent over couches and car seats and tables and countertops.

I've seen her on her knees in alleys while some guy unloads into her mouth. I've seen her with her eyes closed and her eyes open and her mouth sagging open in screams of ecstasy.

I've never seen the way she looks when she wants to tear someone apart, though—until now.

She's actually a stunningly pretty young woman with bouncy blonde curls, a childlike, innocent face, and a small, pert nose that points up at the end.

She has the classic good looks and bombshell figure that can land her any man she wants. She only has to smile at a guy to make him collapse on his knees at her feet—or vice versa.

She obviously turned Judah's head—so why is he interested in me?

I don't even know that he is interested in me. Everything that happened in that bar was totally appropriate to our working relationship. No one would be able to see us doing anything compromising because we didn't do anything compromising.

Maybe it's all in my head that he was implying anything at all. I can brush it off and forget all about it.

I can't do that when I'm face to face with Skyla. "You slut!" she blurts out. "You keep your hands off my husband!"

My jaw drops. I'm almost too shocked to answer. "Your.....what?"

"I saw you in there just now, you filthy bitch!" Her voice rises. Passersby stare at us. "You think you can steal him from me? You keep away from Judah!"

"I....I can't....I'm his lawyer.....his divorce lawyer. He's divorcing you. You aren't married anymore."

"Yes, we are!" she roars. "He's mine! Do you hear me?! I swear if I see you anywhere near him, I'll make you sorry! I saw you making eyes at him and drooling all over him. Do you think I'm blind?!"

I open my mouth to answer, but the sheer insanity of what she's saying stuns me into silence.

I actually have to scramble in my memory to remember if I did anything inappropriate around Judah at all. I touched his arm. That's all.

He looked at me with a lot more obvious desire and passion than I looked at him.

Okay, maybe I can't be in the same room with him without ogling his good looks, but he started it. I wasn't even thinking about him that way until he made it so obvious.

He was the one who looked me up and down and said I was good-looking enough to have a boyfriend. He was the one who said it in a way that made it abundantly clear that he wanted to be that way with me.

He was the one who asked me to have a drink with him and he was the one who touched me first. I didn't do anything to him that he didn't do to me.

Holy shit, that sounds awful! It really sounds like we did something, but we didn't.

Could Skyla see those pulsations of mind-blowing energy coming from him? She must know him well enough to recognize when he wants something—or someone.

Which means she must have been standing close enough to see us.

My mind blasts apart when I realize the truth. "Skyla....did you.... are you stalking Judah?"

"I'm not doing anything except trying to save my marriage from worthless bitches like you! We would be happy if you didn't keep sticking your hands down his pants and luring him away from me."

My throat goes dry. "I never stuck my hands down his pants."

"I saw you!!" she bellows. "I saw you with my own eyes, you filthy slut! You stay away from him, or I swear to God, I'll make you sorry!!"

She storms off down the street. I can only stand in horror and watch her leave. This woman really is batshit crazy if she thinks she saw that.

A few more people give me strange looks and I wake up enough to realize where I am. I'm standing in the middle of the sidewalk staring at nothing. I'm alone. Skyla isn't here.

I shudder and hurry away to call a cab. I have to get back to the office so I can go over Judah's documentation again.

Now I know we're dealing with a completely different breed of cat. If Skyla accused me of that, she's a lot more unstable than I realized.

Chapter 6: Judah

I struggle to slow my pulse on my way upstairs to Piper's office. Why am I getting so excited about seeing her again? All we did was share a drink.

She's so much hotter close up when she isn't acting all businesslike. Sitting right next to her sharing a drink with her and talking makes me feel how attractive and inviting she is.

I want to get my hands on her, but I can't do that. I have to stop myself from getting hard just from thinking about her.

Not only does she have a perfect body under those tight-fitting, classy feminine suits, but she has a personality to match.

She doesn't act biting and hard-driving like most businesswomen. She has a softness and a caring side. She's been so sympathetic to my situation. It makes her irresistible.

I open the door to her office and find her standing in the same place waiting for me. She smiles up at me in genuine warmth and holds out her hand to shake mine, but this meeting is so different from the last one.

This tension between us—it fills the room with palpable strain. Her small, soft hand feels silky and gentle in mine.

I find myself beaming down at her in something like heavenly admiration. "Hello again," I rasp.

"It's good to see you. Come on in and sit down."

Her fingers trail out of mine. The feeling of her skin passing over mine gives me an electric thrill that shoots straight to my crotch.

She wears another tight-cut vintage suit that instantly gives me ideas I shouldn't have. Her eyes glow with sympathy and soft warmth.

Does she even think of me in that way? Probably not. She's my lawyer. Even she says so. Of course she does. That's all she is.

I shouldn't think about her this way, so I sit down in the same chair as last time. She sits down in her chair, but that only brings her cleavage into my line of sight.

I fight back a flood of imagines and fantasies to concentrate on what she's telling me.

"Well, your wife filed a counter-complaint against you. She's seeking..."

"She what?!" I snap. "She....what?!"

"She filed a counter-complaint against you. She's accusing you of infidelity....."

I shoot out of my chair. "She what?!! I never did anything with anyone outside our marriage! She was the one!"

Piper raises both hands and lowers her voice. "I know, Judah. Sit down. Please. This is nothing we shouldn't have expected under the circumstances. Come on, Judah. Sit down."

Her voice saying my name brings me back from the edge of madness—a little bit. Skyla is not accusing me of infidelity. That's impossible.

I stand across the room trying to think. I realize from a distance that I'm glaring at Piper as if she's the one doing this to me.

I should sit down, but I can't move. I want to fight someone to make this not true, but it is true. I see that in the pained sympathy in Piper's eyes.

She sighs and goes on as if I really did sit down. "This is nothing we haven't seen a million times before. She has to come up with this counter-complaint to block your accusation against her."

"But....I never did anything...."

"I know you didn't," she murmurs. "Our next move is to file a motion for discovery. That will force her hand so she has to show any evidence to support her complaint."

I can't stand here listening to this, but I can't leave her office, either. I pace back and forth behind the chairs.

Piper doesn't act like my reaction is anything unusual. I hate that this affects me as much as it does.

At least she's the only one seeing me this upset. I couldn't stand it if anyone from the business world saw me like this.

Piper waits for me to say something else. She lets me pace for a minute and then murmurs, "Sit down, Judah. I need to talk to you about this and I need you to answer my questions as rationally as possible. Can you do that?"

Her soft voice melts my agitation. I can't resist her voice.

I sit down in the chair, but I can't keep still. I keep shifting my weight all over the place and I can't look at her.

She takes another deep breath and checks through some files on her desk. "Skyla claims you had an affair five years ago with a woman in your office—a junior marketing executive by the name of Jasmine Delvini. Does that name ring a bell?"

I groan and cover my eyes. "Yes."

"Did something happen between you two?"

"No, nothing happened between me and Jasmine except that she worked for me for a little while. She was a subordinate to one of my executives, so I hardly ever talked to her. She attended our company Christmas party and Skyla was there. She saw me talking to Jasmine and Skyla freaked out. She started throwing accusations all over the place and accused me of sleeping with Jasmine—but I never did. I never laid a finger on her."

Piper holds up her hand again. "Okay. I believe you. So what happened?"

"Skyla got completely irrational about it. She cornered Jasmine after the party and warmed her to stay away from me. Jasmine quit a month later. I haven't seen her or heard from her since."

Piper only nods. "Okay. I see. That makes sense."

"Why does it make sense? I never did anything with her. I was just talking to her in a totally neutral business setting. Skyla flipped out and went all *Basic Instinct* on Jasmine."

"I'm not saying it makes sense because you did anything. I'm saying it makes sense considering how Skyla is acting now. She confronted me outside the bar yesterday...."

My blood runs cold and I stare at her. "She what?"

"She confronted me outside the bar yesterday after you asked me to have a drink with you. She accused me of.....doing stuff with you....."

I can't even gasp. I can barely whisper. "She did not!"

Piper nods. "She said a lot of things, but it was obvious she was watching us—maybe through the front window....."

"How could she see us when there were so many people in the way?"

"I don't know, but she must have. That's the only way she could have known we were both in there. Anyway, she accused me of throwing myself at you and luring you away from her and she said you would be happy together if I only kept my hands off you...."

I shoot out of my chair even faster. I turn my back to her and pace the room. I am not hearing this.

Skyla did not accuse Piper of any of that. Hell no.

"It doesn't matter because she won't be able to show evidence of infidelity the way you can," Piper goes on. "As soon as we get through the discovery phase, the judge will dismiss her complaint and yours will be left standing."

I stop across the room with my back to her. How can I face Piper with this accusation hanging in the air?

I wanted to. That's the problem. I wanted to do it with her. I might even have made it obvious by the way I was looking at her. I wanted to do a lot of things with her.

All those things rush into my mind right now, but I can't say or even act on them. Piper is out of my reach. Maybe she always will be.

That doesn't matter because I brought this on her. I brought Skyla into her life. Skyla made those accusations against Piper because of me.

I can't even think that Skyla is trying to hurt me through Piper. Skyla doesn't know how I feel about Piper. I don't even know how I feel about Piper.

I do know how I feel about Piper and I showed her at the bar. I showed her by the way I looked at her and the way I said she was good-looking.

If Skyla was anywhere near enough to see us, she would have seen that. She knows me too well not to recognize that look.

"Judah...." Piper murmurs.

That voice curls around me in a blanket of warmth. I feel her skin all over me.....her mouth tasting me.....her tongue kissing me......her legs spreading for me.....That voice says it all. It breathes with so many unspoken possibilities.

She pushes her chair back. I don't turn around. I follow her movements with my ears.

She walks around her desk and comes up behind me. Is she about to put her arms around me from behind? Is she about to touch me and set off this chain reaction that will blow us both apart?

"Listen to me, Judah," she murmurs even lower. "You can't take this personally. You can't take everything she does as a personal insult. I'm really starting to believe she's out of her mind. She thinks she can still get you back. She still thinks you're her husband and that you two are just working through some stuff before you get back together. You can't take what she says to heart. You'll drive yourself crazy doing that."

I turn around extra slowly. I have to measure every move I make because Piper is standing this close to me. How did I start feeling this way about her so fast?

"You don't believe this, do you, Piper?" I ask. "You don't believe I actually did this. Tell me you don't."

She spreads both hands and shrugs. "It isn't my place to believe or not. I learned a long time ago not to believe anything in this business. Whatever happened between you and Jasmine isn't part of my job."

I groan and turn away again. So she does believe it. I had one person I could talk to—one person who believed I was the wronged party in this. Skyla even managed to rob me of that.

Piper puts out her hand to touch my arm again. It's such a caring, sensitive move, but she stops herself from actually touching me. She must realize by now that it would mean more than just showing she cares.

Even her hesitation shows she cares. She doesn't want to trespass.

"Sit down," she murmurs. "I need to go over some of your assets with you."

She motions toward the chairs. When I still don't move, she circles her desk and sits down in her own place. She waits for me to do the same thing.

I drag myself over there and collapse in my seat, but the shock is starting to wear off.

So Skyla confronted Piper on the street outside the bar. That bitch!

I'll just have to straighten her out. Cheating on me is one thing. I can't have her going around slinging accusations at every woman I have a conversation with.

Piper goes through her files for a minute. "I've been meaning to ask you about this listing in your trust assets. I don't understand the nomenclature."

"What is it?" I ask.

"That's what I'm asking you." She bends over the file and reads out, "This one says 49SK-29B...and this one says 20DF-96C. What does that mean?"

"Oh." My brain finally clears. "They're diamonds."

Her head shoots up and she stares at me. "Excuse me?"

"Diamonds—loose diamonds. They aren't set in any jewelry or anything. They're just loose stones."

"What do you have them for?"

"I collect them—just like Skyla collects stuffed animals. I research different stones, and when I find one I want, I buy it. These are in a vault in Antwerp."

She takes extra long staring at me. "You....you collect diamonds."

"It's a hobby...and an investment. It's both."

She clears her throat and straightens up. "Oh. Okay. So.....does Skyla know about this?"

"Nope. She doesn't know I have them at all. I started collecting before I met her and I never told her. In fact, I've never told any-one—except you. That's why I use a code for each stone in the documentation—for an added layer of security. This way, if anyone sees the documents, they won't know I have them."

Her eyes go glassy again. Does she realize now how much I'm depending on her?

If Skyla somehow found out about those diamonds, she would do absolutely anything to get them.

I don't see how she could have found out. I never bought any diamonds or even looked at any diamonds when she was around. I suppose anything is possible, though.

Piper shakes herself and turns to another page of a different file. "This listing states that you purchased an apartment building at 3078-83rd Street two years ago—while you were married to Skyla."

"Yeah. What about it?"

"If you purchased it in your own name and then transferred it to the trust, Skyla could claim that it was joint marital property even for a few minutes or however long it was in your name. That could give her a claim on the asset."

"It was never in my name because I didn't purchase it. The trust did. That's exactly why I do it this way. Besides, my daily operating account never has enough money in it for me to make a purchase that big. The money would have to go out of the trust." I lean forward in my chair and flip to a different file. "If you check the purchase agreement, you'll see that the purchaser was the trust, not me."

"Of course. I see that now. And....." She hesitates again. "The accounts for your North Star Investment Consultation Service indicate four additional payments to Jasmine Delvini after she quit. What are those about?"

"She was working with a client when she quit. The client wanted to keep working with her to finish the project even after Jasmine left the company. We paid her to work for us on a per diem basis just until she finished the project."

"So you did talk to her after she quit. You said earlier that you never saw or heard from her again."

I stiffen at her tone. Piper better not be interrogating me about Jasmine. "I didn't see or hear from her again. The marketing executive who was her boss dealt with her and coordinated all her meetings with the client. Our accounting department handled payment. I had nothing to do with any of it or with Jasmine after that Christmas party. It was the last time I ever laid eyes on her."

She nods at me across the desk, but I sense the words bouncing right off her. This accusation changes things—if there was ever anything to change.

If she responded to me at all yesterday, that's all gone now. She closes up in front of me like a locked box—just from the insinuation that I might have cheated.

Whatever happened to her must have been bad. Now she has to protect herself even from the hint that it might happen again.

Chapter 7: Judah

I spot Skyla walking down the street ahead. I'm riding in the back seat of a rented Bentley so she doesn't recognize my limo.

My driver motors up behind her so she doesn't see me coming. The driver pulls over to the curb and I jump out half a block behind her.

The Bentley drives off to circle the block while I walk up behind Skyla.

"Hey!" I snap. "Skyla!"

She spins around and stops in her tracks when she sees me.

She's wearing old clothes that look like they came from a secondhand store. She's still wearing the same makeup she wore when we were married, but she didn't take as much care to put it on this morning. It makes her look older.

She gasps out, "Judah!" and actually starts to smile like she thinks I came to take her back or some bullshit.

"How dare you accost Piper Lagrange on the street?!" I fire back. "Don't ever let me find out you went anywhere near her again. Do you hear me? She's my lawyer, Skyla. Do you understand that? We aren't seeing each other and it wouldn't be any of your business if we were, I'm just working with her. Don't go near her again. You can say whatever you want about me, but don't even talk to her. Don't let her see your face. Is that clear?"

Her face goes through a rapid series of expressions. She finally takes a step toward me and tries to put on the wheedling charm. "I only wanted to get you back, Judah! I love you! There has to be a way to work this out somehow."

"How do you plan to work it out that you took it from more than thirty guys—and those are just the ones I know about. You must have seen the folder of video clips by now. Do you think I could ever work it out with you after that?"

"You don't understand. I was only trying to be sexy like you wanted me to be..."

"With me!" I hear my voice rising. "I wanted you to be like that with me—not with every other guy in the county."

"It wasn't like that." She starts whining. "Come on, Judah. You have to forgive me. You know I never cared about any of those guys. I love you."

"It was very much like that. You nailed some guy in my own house. Do you think I could ever forgive you for that?"

"You can't blame me for getting jealous. I saw the way you looked at that slut...."

"Don't you dare!" I hiss. "Don't you dare call her a slut! She is a professional. You're the only slut here, Skyla."

She takes one more step closer to me. Her presence turns my stomach. I automatically recoil from her and retreat out of range.

Her expression changes in a flash. Her lower lip starts to tremble, but just as fast, she clamps her mouth shut tight, glares at me, and snarls at me, "If you ever touch her, I swear I'll make sure you pay for it."

"I'm paying for it already just by living on the same planet with you. Don't go near her again. She's handling my side of the divorce. That's all. Don't get yourself in even more trouble than you're already in by making this worse."

I stalk past her just as the Bentley comes around the corner behind me. She calls out, "Judah! Come back! I love you! I can make it right! I know I can! Just give me a second chance!"

I pull open the car door, climb inside, and the car speeds away with me in it.

My heart won't stop pounding. Skyla better not try to pull anything else on Piper.

Protective rage eats through my guts at the thought. Piper is too good to do anything like that. She would never cross that line. It took a lot for me to even convince her to have a drink with me.

She's been nothing but supportive and kind to me. She doesn't deserve this, especially when she's obviously gotten hurt in the past.

I kick myself for bringing this drama into her life. She doesn't need this because my ex is a psychotic witch.

I cringe when I think about what Skyla must have said to her. Piper glossed it over, but it must have been bad.

I wish Piper would put her hands on me. I wish she would do a lot of things to me just like I wish I could do a lot of things to her.

I could never do that to her, though. I respect her too much. Her integrity to her job is the thing I respect most about her. I couldn't trample that by even implying that she compromise it.

The Bentley driver drops me off at the Citicorp Building downtown where I get into my own limo and go to the office. I have too much to do to think about Skyla or Piper or my divorce.

God, I hate that word! Divorce. It sounds so tasteless and low-class.

I head upstairs to my office and bend over my laptop to check my other appointments for the day. I have three other meetings this afternoon. I've already wasted enough time on my personal life.

One of my appointments today is with Kevin Drake and Rory Khan of The Billionaires' Club. I'm the club's events coordinator. We're supposed to talk about holding a memorial service for Miles Reynolds, a member who recently passed away.

Just then, Marcus Jeffries, my CFO, comes in. "The Board of Directors is asking to see you immediately, Judah."

I look up. "They are? Why? I never heard about this."

"They called an emergency meeting of the whole executive. We're all going. We just found out about it an hour ago."

I frown at him. "Um...okay. I guess so."

I give instructions to my assistant to rearrange my schedule. This meeting with the directors better be something exceptional if they want to interfere with my commitments like this.

I follow Marcus across the executive floor. I've been working here long enough to sense when something isn't right.

The place hums with tension. People whisper in their cubicles. Are they whispering about me or just because all the executives got called to an emergency meeting with the Board of Directors?

Marcus enters the boardroom first. I follow him. I'm the last one to show up. This can't be good.

The rest of my executive team already sits at the table. They sit with the directors—which means this is about me. Even Marcus sits down.

I remain standing. If I'm going to face the firing squad, I'll damn well do it on my feet.

I swivel to the chair at the other end of the table. It's the only empty chair left. "What's this about?" I ask. I hope I don't sound too defensive or demanding even though I am.

"The story just broke out on the internet," Maxwell Frost, the board chairman tells me. "Some reporter got hold of your estranged wife's divorce filings. The whole world is talking about you having an affair with Jasmine Delvini."

I clamp my lips shut. I don't even stoop to deny the accusation. The board better come up with something better than this if they want to make my life difficult.

"We need to talk about this, Judah," the vice-chairman, Dennis Hutton adds. "We need to do damage control before this gets out of hand."

"If you have anything to say to us, say it now, Judah," Marcus chimes in. "We need to know everything you know so we can handle this the best way."

I look back and forth from one man to another. I don't say a word. I didn't wake up this morning to deal with this shit.

"Don't you have anything to say about this at all?" Maxwell asks. "This could destroy your career—and all of ours. Our investors won't stand for any impropriety."

"I don't have anything to say because there is no impropriety," I snap. "There never has been and there never will be anything going on between me and Jasmine Delvini. You all know this as well as I do. My psycho ex made this up to get back at me because I busted her sleeping around. Nothing happened between me and Jasmine. As soon as these reporters follow up on that and ask her, they'll find out the truth and all of this will blow over."

"We don't need this kind of publicity," Dennis breaks in. "Can't you just settle with your ex and make all of this go away?"

"If I settle with her, it will never go away. I'll be admitting that something happened between me and Jasmine when it didn't. I didn't do anything with Jasmine and I won't settle. This accusation is false and it will be proven false. Honestly, guys, if this is the worst problem we face running this company, we'll be lucky."

"I wish I could share your careless attitude about this, Judah...." Maxwell begins.

"Careless!" I fire back. "Careless! Do you actually think I don't care that some skank is out there smearing my reputation and spreading lies about me all over the country?!"

"Please, Judah," Marcus murmurs. "There's no need for that kind of language in here."

"No, there's a need for much worse language. She's hurting me a hell of a lot worse than she's hurting you or the company. If the company can't back me up and support me when I need it, then we're going to start having a serious issue. I built this company from nothing. Everything that happens here happens because of me. Neither you nor she nor anyone else on the planet can show a single shred of proof that I had more than one conversation with Jasmine Delvini. I think I've earned a little more support than this from the board and from the executive team. Now you've all forced me to reschedule an important meeting I had this afternoon. I won't let you ruin the rest of my day with unfounded, malicious accusations with no basis in fact. If you don't have anything else you want to talk about, we're done here."

No one says anything when I walk out. The nerve of these people!

This accusation better not start following me around everywhere I go. I have better things to do with my life.

I go back to my office for a while. I have a break since my assistant had to reschedule my first meeting.

He comes back ten minutes later. "Kevin Drake, Rory Khan, and Jackson Metcalf are here to see you."

"Jackson! What's he doing here? He wasn't supposed to be involved in this."

"He didn't explain it to me. They're in the south conference room."

I leave to go meet the other billionaires from the club. My assistant would normally sit in on a meeting like this. He'll be deeply involved in helping me organize the memorial service.

Something tells me to get rid of him, though. I want to see my friends without him listening in.

I tell him to take a break and I enter the conference room alone. The three other billionaires come forward to greet me and shake hands.

Rory is the youngest man here with dark brown hair, brooding dark eyes, and a deep, watchful personality. He's a mystery to everyone, but he's as sharp as they come and he can read people in one look.

He's only thirty and he runs a multi-billion-dollar corporate talent agency worldwide. He doesn't mess around with staffing at the lower levels. That's Kevin's thing.

Rory handles executive and higher-level employment positions that are almost impossible to hire for. He's an expert at finding exactly the right person for exactly the right position.

My company has used his service many times and he always sends us the right people.

He knows everyone—as in everyone on the planet. I have never met anyone anywhere in any walk of life who didn't know him—which is strange considering how reserved and quiet he can be.

"How you doing?" Kevin begins, but he doesn't mean it like that. It's just something to say.

"I'm fine," I reply. "Did we decide on a date for the memorial service?"

Jackson clamps his hand on my shoulder. "Slow down, man. We can all see you're steamed about something."

I start to protest and immediately give it up. These guys know me better than anyone. Of course they can tell when something is bothering me.

"Is it the divorce?" Rory asks. "Shit, I wouldn't wish your situation on my worst enemy."

"Thanks, man," I growl under my breath. "I really wish I could just forget about it for like an hour. I don't ask much. Just an hour."

"Do you want us to give you some time?" Kevin asks. "We can do this later if you need to."

"No, I want to get it done now. I just...." I shouldn't complain about this to them, but they're the only people I have to talk to about this. "My Board of Directors just called me in about my ex's accusation against me. There's no evidence. It's just....it gets to me."

"Of course it does," Rory replies. "It would get to anyone."

I open my mouth to launch into the story about Skyla accusing Piper, but I stop myself from saying that. I can't talk about Piper—ever.

That's the moment when I realize she means something to me. Don't ask me what she means. I couldn't define it if I tried.

I care what she thinks. I actually care that she's holding me at a distance because of this accusation. I could live with anything else, but not that.

Why does she matter to me so much? Am I so desperate for some woman to validate that I'm worth considering? Did Skyla really emasculate me that much?

I can't let Piper become that. I can't let her become some crutch I use to make myself feel better. I couldn't do that to her or to myself.

Chapter 8: Piper

I check the directions on my phone and hustle down the sidewalk getting closer to Skyla's mother's house.

Judah said he sent Skyla's stuffed animal collection here. Skyla also used this as the mailing address for her counter-complaint in the divorce.

I know Skyla is staying here because I've seen her here before. I need more information about her that I can't get from any of the documentation.

I'm still almost a full block away from the address when Skyla comes out of the house. I stop in my tracks to watch her, but she doesn't see me.

She crosses to the curb just as a big black Cadillac pulls up in front of her. The tires have been set farther out from the fenders than normal. The tires give the vehicle a gangster look.

Someone calls to Skyla from inside and she replies. She crosses to the passenger window, bends in, and arches her back to stick out her ass while she talks to someone in the car.

She looks more like a streetwalker than ever like this. Is this how she supports herself since she threw Judah in the trash? Damn. She really downgraded in life.

She holds a short conversation with the driver, laughs, and sets off walking down the street heading away from me. She's wearing sweatpants and a hoodie, so she can't be out here turning tricks.

The Cadillac purrs along keeping level with her while the guy keeps trying to talk to her. She laughs a few more times and waves him away before the vehicle drives off.

She keeps going and turns a corner. I hurry after her. Where is she going? What is she doing? It's five o'clock in the afternoon.

I've checked out her activities five other times. She never goes anywhere during the day. She just stays in the house.

She walks fast like she needs to get somewhere. Does she have a night job or something?

I make it as far as the corner and spot her farther down the street. I tail her for another seven blocks.

I stand on the opposite corner and stare in slack-jawed amazement when she turns into a strip club in a terrible part of town.

Real streetwalkers slouch on the corners outside. A bunch of drug dealers wearing baggy pants and baseball caps stuck sideways on their heads strut back and forth accosting passersby.

Skyla did not just go into a strip club. Is that where she's working?

There could be a perfectly logical explanation for this. She could be washing dishes in the back. This could be perfectly innocent.

Something tells me that might be asking too much, though. I cross the street and approach the bouncer at the door.

He stops me. "Where do you think you're going?"

"I'm looking for someone." I show him a picture of Skyla. "I just saw her come in here. I need to talk to her."

He furrows his brow at me. "You aren't a client. We only let paying clients inside."

"Please. It's important. I need to talk to her about a financial settlement she's involved in. If it works out in her favor, she could get a lot of money. I just need to see her. Can't you make an exception? I won't cause any trouble. I swear."

He scowls at me and then gives in. "Fine. Just make it quick and don't let any of the customers see you. Women in the club make them uncomfortable."

I don't know about that. I've been in plenty of strip clubs with women customers. None of the men seemed to have any problem with it. That sounds like an excuse to get rid of me, but he lets me in anyway.

I cross the threshold into a shadow vestibule. A bead curtain separates me from the main club floor.

Colored strobe lights shine through the beads and cast the only light into the vestibule. I can see the stage through the curtain.

A girl in chaps and nothing else dances in slow gyrations on the stage. A bunch of guys sit in chairs beneath her. Only half the guys even seem to be paying attention to the show.

No one notices me step through the curtain and approach a grizzly guy polishing the glasses behind the bar.

I hold up Skyla's picture. "Can you tell me where I can find this girl? I need to talk to her."

He points toward the stage. "Through the door marked, 'Fire Exit', down the hall, past the bathrooms, and through the door marked, 'Private'."

I don't know what that means, but I follow his directions. I pass through the door marked, *Fire Exit,* and enter a long, dim hall. My shoes stick to the floor with every step.

A bunch of couples line the hall. Some of the girls kneel on the floor sucking the guys while the guys pump into their mouths. Other guys bang the girls against the walls either from the front or from behind.

Screams, grunts, and moans fill the hall. This is not what I expected to find in a strip club, but I don't see Skyla anywhere.

I have to push my way between the couples. One guy thrusting into a girl's mouth gives me a dirty look over his shoulder. Then he bellows as he slams all the way down the girl's throat. He holds her by the hair and she swallows rapidly to keep up with him.

I do my best not to look too closely at anything else. I shoulder my way to the door marked, *Private.* I can't imagine why anyone would care about being private after what's going on out here in the hall. No one is trying to be private here.

I push the door open and enter another hall. This one is bright with glowing pastel colors coming from both sides.

The area behind that door has been divided into small rooms separated by curtains. The light shimmers through the curtains so no one can really see what's going on in any other room.

No one can block the sound, though. The same surging tide of voices screaming, moaning, whimpering, and growling comes from all sides.

I hear men talking dirty and encouraging people to take it deep and hard and a bunch of other things I don't want to repeat.

I glance into the first little room. A girl lies on her back with a guy straddling her head. He clamps her hair in one fist, pins her head to the floor, and pumps into her mouth. He gasps with every thrust.

I look away and spot another girl on all fours with a guy kneeling behind her. He holds her by the hair while he slams into her hard enough to make her scream.

I inch farther down the hall. Is Skyla really in here turning tricks with these guys? Why am I even surprised?

I just hate to think how Judah will react when he finds out. I have to tell him. He deserves to know the truth.

I pass another room on my left where a girl lies on her back with her legs spread. Her customer buries his face between her legs and she holds onto his hair while she writhes and contorts on his mouth.

A girl in the next room on the right straddles her customer riding him. He lies on his back with his arms and legs spread and tied down as far out as they'll go.

The girl holds onto a belt strapped around his neck. She pulls it extra hard each time she grinds on him.

I'm barely holding it together seeing all this. I need to get the hell out of here before I lose my mind, but when I come to the next room, I stop in my tracks.

Skyla bends over propping her hands against the room's back wall. It's the only solid wall in the place. She turns to look over her shoulder so I can see that it really is her.

The guy behind her stands with his legs spread. His ass contracts each time he drives into her. He holds her by both hips and snarls through gritted teeth.

Her blonde curls and her breasts and ass bounce exactly the way they did in the video clip from Judah's house. She throws back her head and moans with her eyes closed. She has exactly the same facial expression. She's enjoying this.

I don't need to see any more. I stride back out to the hall, shove my way through all the couples outside the bathroom, and back to the strip club.

I go over to the bartender. "Did you find her?" he asks.

I nod. "How long has she been working here?"

"Oh, I'd say about six years. She's one of our best. Plenty of guys only come here for her. She brings in more money than all the others combined."

I do my best not to show any sign of surprise. Why am I surprised? She's been turning tricks here the whole time she's been married to Judah. Poor guy. Don't even ask me how I'm going to tell him.

Chapter 9: Judah

I keep it serious when I step into Piper's office. "Hi," I murmur.

"Thank you for coming in. Take a seat."

She waves to the chairs and sits down behind her desk, but I can tell this is different—again. Something must have happened—something bad.

I don't want to sit down. I want to stay standing. I feel more like I'm facing the firing squad here than in the company boardroom. "What happened? What's going on?"

She looks up at me and seems to decide not to push it. She folds her hands on the desk and takes a deep breath to work up her courage. "I'm really sorry to be the one who has to tell you this, but Skyla is a prostitute—a real one. She makes her money by turning tricks at a strip club in the Bronx. She's been doing it for six years—the whole time she's been married to you."

I stare at her trying to comprehend what she just said. Now I'm really glad I didn't sit down.

I shouldn't be surprised by this. I guess I'm just surprised that I didn't see it coming.

I turn aside and start pacing again. I can't feel anything—no anger, no sadness, no nothing. I feel dead inside.

"I checked her employment records," Piper goes on. "She's been using an assumed name to hide what she's been doing. She's had hundreds of clients over the years—some of them repeat customers who come back every week just to see her. Apparently she's really good at what she does."

I stop across the room and stare at the wall. Those words bounce right off me.

Piper isn't talking about anyone I could ever be married to. She's talking about some stranger—someone I've never met. I can't accept this any other way.

"I got the client list and there are some very wealthy, powerful men on it. I think you should take a look at it. I think you owe it to yourself to find out who you might have been doing business with who might have gotten mixed up with her behind your back."

Those words snap me out of my trance. I turn to face her, and like magic, she rotates her laptop toward me so I can see the screen.

The screen shows a spreadsheet with dozens of names on it—male names. I don't recognize most of them.

I scroll down the page and come to a dozen that she's highlighted to make them stand out.

Peirce Robbins.

Timothy Spader.

Verner Smith.

They're all members of The Billionaires' Club.

"Do you know them?" she asks.

I nod at nothing, straighten up, and turn away. I need to get out of this office. I need to get away from Piper and everyone else alive.

I need to go off alone somewhere—somewhere I can process this new outrage.

Finding out that she cheated and even finding her in my house with another man didn't hit me this hard.

This explains why other club members were laughing at me behind my back. I just didn't know they'd been doing it for so long.

They knew. They must have known. They've all seen me with Skyla, either in public or at club functions where wives and dates are invited.

These men knew who she was and they did it with her anyway. They did it with her multiple times—maybe even hundreds or thousands of times.

I don't seem to be able to leave Piper's office, even though I know I need to. I stop there staring at nothing.

This is the only place in the world where I can deal with this information. She's the only person who's here for me. No one else can be here for me because no one else knows about this.

She comes over to me, lays her hand on my arm, squeezes, and this time, she doesn't let go. "I'm really sorry to tell you this, but there's more. Skyla filed another counter-complaint—an addendum to the first one. She's accusing you of infidelity—with me."

My head shoots up and I stare at her.

Piper gazes up at me with such clear, reassuring eyes. She doesn't act surprised or hurt or even angry. Why should she when she knows the accusation is false?

I actually feel honored that Skyla thinks I could do it with Piper. I really wish I could. Having an affair with her would be a privilege, a privilege I'll never get to enjoy. That window is closed to me now.

She slides her hand behind me, down my back in a perfectly innocent, comforting stroke, and lowers her arm. "Can I do anything for you? Can I drive you home or something? I don't think you should go out there alone right now."

I look down at my hands. They don't belong to me anymore.

I don't know what to say to her. Words don't even begin to cut it.

She cocks her head to one side and studies me for a minute. Then she takes my arm and tugs me toward her desk. "Come here and sit down."

I follow her there and she pushes me into a chair. She sits back down at her desk and talks to me while she works on her computer.

"I've just been going over some of the records from the club where she works. They have rooms in the back where the girls work, but the same club also sends out the girls to visit clients in their homes or other locations on request. We can't get video footage from the club, but we might be able to get it from other places. If we can get it, we might be able to subpoena the clients to testify on your behalf—or at least to testify that they hired her. I'm also trying to get in touch with Jasmine Delvini. I'm sure she'll be as enthusiastic about clearing the air as you a re."

Those words sink a little deeper into my brain. Club. Guys from The Billionaires' Club paid Skyla to do it with them.

I can never show my face there again. I can never set foot in The Billionaires' Club again as long as I live.

I know who my friends are. I'll keep doing business with them. I'll never look sideways at anyone on this list—not ever again.

I pull out my phone and send Kevin Drake a text. *I'm withdrawing from the club. You need to find someone else to run the memorial service. I'm out.*

I hit, *Send,* and put my phone away. I feel better now. I don't know why.

I had to break something and it was this. The Billionaires' Club has been my social outlet for years. Now that's gone, too.

Skyla doesn't need to take my money. She's ruined everything else in my life. She might as well take that, too. What the hell do I care anymore?

I look up to find Piper studying me. "Are you okay?" she asks.

I nod at nothing. "I better go."

She stands up and walks around the desk to accompany me to the door. She's so small and slim and tight. I want to put my arms around her. I want to hold her.

I want to feel that connection that we're in this together, but she doesn't want that. I don't want to alienate her when she's doing so much to help me.

I pause on the threshold to face her. "Thank you," I murmur.

She raises her tiny, delicate hand and runs it up and down my arm. I feel enormous next to her. "We'll get through this. It will pass."

I stare down into her eyes. She really believes that. She just said, *we*. We're in this together.

I want to tell her so many things. I can't leave her office without saying something.

"You know..." I rasp. "It's a massive compliment that she thinks there could ever be anything between us."

She turns bright red. Then she smiles and giggles. "You're sweet. I feel the same way about you."

My stomach flips at those words. She feels the same way about me.

"I can't imagine anyone pushing you away like this," she goes on. "You're a prize. Maybe that's why she did it. Maybe she's so far removed from you that you repelled each other like polar opposite magnets. That force pushed her back to her side of the tracks and you to yours. Maybe that's what this is all about."

I nod at nothing. I should be more articulate right now.

Piper actually called me a prize.

I want to tell her that she's one, too. Some guy is gonna snap her up one of these days. When he does, he won't ever let her go.

She'll probably do the same thing. She'll find someone and give him everything. Lucky bastard.

Just then, my phone buzzes. It's Kevin. *What happened? Can you meet me to talk about it? Please don't leave because of this. Whatever you need to make it possible for you to stay, you only have to tell me. We need you and I don't mean as our events coordinator. Please don't leave. Please meet me and at least talk to me about it. That's all I ask. Are you busy tonight?*

I don't want to talk about it, but I guess I owe him an explanation. I text back. *How about seven o'clock at the club?*

I don't want to go back there, but meeting there will be better than meeting at some other location. It seems somehow fitting that I go back there to end it.

He replies that he'll be there and I put my phone away. Piper stands there waiting. She's so pure. Everything she does is totally straight up and forthright.

I can't imagine her doing anything dishonest or even concealing anything. It isn't in her nature.

She places her hand on my back and rubs up and down. That touch feels so comforting because it comes from her. I couldn't accept it from anyone else.

She doesn't mean anything by it. A touch like that never communicates any subtext. It's just pure comforting support.

"Let me know if you need anything or if I can do anything for you," she tells me. "This would be hard on anybody. You're in shock right now, but you'll be all right. You're strong enough to come out of this."

I somehow manage to say, "Thank you," again. Her words and reassurance mean so much because I know she's right.

She understands me. She knows I'll come out of this as soon as I start thinking clearly.

She guides me to the door and I walk downstairs where I get into the limo. It takes me a while to remember where I'm going.

"Where to, Sir?" the driver asks.

"The Billionaires' Club," I tell him and we drive away.

Chapter 10: Judah

I use my keys to let myself into The Billionaires' Club. The big main room is empty and silent. No one is here.

The sound of the fountain tinkling and the artificial indoor stream bubbling over its rocky bed fills the silence. I don't hear anyone in the kitchen, either. The staff must have gone home for the night.

I walk through the empty main room, past the pool tables, and into the back office.

I don't usually come in here. This is Jackson's domain. He handles the club's operations. Dante is club president. Kevin handles membership and Rory is responsible for PR.

I trust them all—especially after not seeing their names on Skyla's client list. I expected to see Giovanni Nowaczyk on it. He's such a player. He doesn't care which bimbo he smashes as long as he smashes something.

He isn't on it, though. Maybe he has a shred of common decency after all.

I sit down at the desk and bring up the club's security camera feeds. If these morons are fool enough to bang my wife in some Bronx strip club, they just might be stupid enough to do it here.

I can just picture them bringing her here to show off—or her asking them to bring her here. She would want some of that luxury to rub off on her cheap ass.

I speed through hours upon hours of footage. I skip the parts where a bunch of us are standing around the main room shooting the breeze with each other. She won't be there.

I concentrate on the other areas of the clubs—the bathrooms, the hallways, the kitchens, the indoor gym, the movie theater—anywhere out of sight.

I find what I'm looking for on five different feeds. I locate at least ten incidents each where Peirce Robbins, Tim Spader, and Verner Smits did it with her somewhere on the club premises.

I copy each incident onto a memory stick, transfer the footage to one of the club's laptops. I finish ten minutes before seven.

I shut down the system and go back to the main room just as Kevin shows up. He brings Jackson, Lane, and Dante with him. I didn't expect that.

Kevin walks right up to me and shakes my hand. "Thank you for coming in to talk to us. I really hope we can work this out."

I don't say anything. The others gather around me in a circle.

"What is this about?" Lane asks. "What made you decide to quit all of a sudden?"

"If it's about your divorce...." Dante begins.

"It isn't about my divorce. It's about the club itself. I just found out my ex has been turning tricks in some dive in the Bronx and servicing club members on the side the whole time we've been married. These people know who she is and they stuck it to her anyway. I don't see how I can stay a member with this going on."

Dante's jaw drops. "You can't be serious."

"I can prove it."

"How can you prove it?" Jackson asks. "Your ex is hostile toward you. She won't vouch for you."

"I don't need her to vouch for me. I have the proof right here." I hold up the memory stick.

"What is that?" Lane asks.

"I just told you. It's the proof that these people have been screwing around with my wife behind my back. They've even been doing it on club premises."

"We have to see this proof," Kevin tells me.

"That's why I brought it." I plug the stick into the laptop and play back the footage.

The four of them stand there staring as I go through each incident. Some of these incidents occurred while the other members were right outside in the main room.

The only miracle is that none of them got caught before now. I guess no one goes over the security feed on a regular basis. They don't need to if nothing ever happens.

Kevin turns away first, passes his hand across his mouth, and whispers, "Jesus."

Lane stands there staring at the laptop in stunned silence. Dante glares at it.

Good old Jackson storms right up to me. "You can't quit, man. We need you too bad. You're better than this. We'll get rid of them. We'll boot every one of them. Just stay. Please."

"He's right," Lane husks under his breath. "We can't let them stay in the club—not after this." He looks up and around at the others. "Come on, Kevin. There has to be some stipulation we can use to kick them out. We can't let them screw over one of their fellow members without some consequence. We have to get rid of them. They could do the same thing to any of us."

"I agree," Dante chimes in. "None of the guys' wives will be safe—and none of the guys will feel safe to belong to the club if they think the other members are going to cannibalize their wives. It could drive away future members if anyone found out. We have to cut these guys."

"Who else is there besides there three—Pierce, Tim, and Vern?" Jackson asks. "Are these the only ones?"

I shrug. "As far as I know."

"Will you stay if we drop-kick them out of the club?" he insists. "Come on, man. Let the rest of us do the right thing. Don't ditch all of us because of a few bad apples. Give us a chance to make it right."

I hesitate. I don't want to. I don't want to trust that the club is as good as I originally thought. This bad experience colors my whole view of it and all the members, even the good ones.

"We'll throw them out even if you do leave," Kevin finally agrees. "We have to. We can't let this slide."

"How will we do it?" Dante asks. "The club bylaws don't include anything like this."

"The club's mission is to provide a supportive environment where billionaires can network and collaborate with each other in the spirit of friendship and mutual benefit. These guys undermined that. If we can't count on each other for support, where else are we supposed to turn? It's hard enough for people in our income bracket to make friends. The club is supposed to provide that and these guys violated that trust. They made the club an unsafe environment for everybody, not just Judah. I think that qualifies them for expulsion."

Dante nods. "That's perfect." He looks up at me. "Does that satisfy you? Whatever you need, just tell us. We don't want to lose you."

"Yeah," Lane adds. "You've been there for all of us. Let us return the favor by having your back now."

Their support means everything. I can only mumble, "All right. Thank you."

Jackson squeezes my shoulder. "You're too important to this club. I only wish we knew about this before. Nothing like this ever should have happened. We need to make an example of these guys so everyone gets the message."

"You should be there," Lane suggests. "You should be present, but we should be the ones who do the actual talking. We'll be the ones to tell them that this has nothing to do with you. We'll tell them that we'd be kicking them out even if you quit the club."

"I don't want to be the one to tell them," I reply. "That would sound too much like I was taking revenge on them."

"No, of course you can't be the one to tell them," Kevin adds. "That's my job—mine, Jackson's, and Dante's. You can just stand there as our mascot."

I murmur, "Thanks," again. I can barely contain the gratitude overwhelming me right now. I didn't expect this kind of support.

I don't know what I expected. I should have expected these guys to back me up all the way. They always do.

Chapter 11: Piper

I stroll through Central Park admiring the autumn leaves changing colors. The beauty of nature somehow wipes away all the smut and horror of the city beyond these trees.

I can forget all my cases here. I'm not a lawyer. I'm just a person walking under the trees.

The fresh hair clears my head. I actually feel happy here.

I meander down the sidewalk heading deeper into the park. I pause when I see Judah coming toward me.

He starts to smile and breaks it off. "Hello," he greets me in his low, sultry voice.

I burst into a grin. "Hey! You actually look alive this time. I knew you'd bounce back."

"Thank you for looking out for me. I really appreciate it."

"Hey, what are friends for, right? No one deserves what you've been through. It was the least I could do."

"Hardly. I don't even want to know what you had to do to find out that information."

I look away. "No, you don't."

I feel him studying me. "You look good," he remarks. "You look...kinda happy."

I grin at him. "I won't take that to mean what I'm pretty sure you didn't mean for it to mean. I do have a life outside the office."

"No, you don't. Don't lie."

I burst out laughing and he grins for the first time. He still tries too hard to hold it back. He does his best to stay serious.

"At least I'm not collecting stuffed animals yet," I tell him. "I still have some self-respect left."

"You aren't turning tricks for a living in the Bronx, either," he replies. "You could do a lot worse."

I shoot him a sidelong glance and keep walking. He walks next to me.

I find myself glancing around to see if anyone is watching us, but we aren't doing anything. We're just walking through the park as lawyer and client.

Judah surveys the park on all sides, too. "I keep expecting you to drop some other bomb on me."

"No more bombs. I think we used up our supply of ammunition."

He smiles again. "That's good. Maybe I can start to rebuild now."

"You won't have any problem. You got where you are. You still have your work and your wealth. You'll be fine."

"I'm glad someone thinks so."

He murmurs it under his breath like he doesn't want me to hear his worst fears.

I want to take his hand—or do something to reassure and support him, but I can't do that. Skyla already accused him of cheating with me.

She also accused him of cheating with Jasmine. That should warn me away from him, but I can't believe that about him.

I want to believe more than anything that he's telling the truth and nothing happened between him and Jasmine.

If it didn't, then I have no reason to keep my distance—apart from the fact that he's my client.

I can't go there, but it sure is nice to think about. He feels big and strong and protective standing next to me. I could get lost in him.

His body doesn't radiate the kind of ravenous power I felt in the bar. This whole catastrophic divorce has tempered him.

Maybe he realizes now that he's in no state to do anything with anyone—not until he puts his life back together.

He sure is hot, though. I have to stop myself from gawking at his magnificent face, domed skull, strong neck, and the square cut of his shoulders under his suit.

I'll start imagining doing all kinds of crazy things with him if I start thinking about his body under that suit. I've never seen it and I probably never will. That's probably a good thing.

We walk past the duck pond and pause on the bridge to look down at the water.

"Why don't you have a boyfriend?" he asks. "It can't be because you aren't good-looking enough. That's nonsense. Tell me the real reason. You got cheated on, didn't you? Tell me what happened. You know the worst about me."

I can't look at him when I tell him. I do know the worst thing about him.

"I didn't have a boyfriend. I had a husband....and he didn't cheat. He was a high school teacher and he was really good. He really cared about the kids. He spent hours after school coaching them and helping them straighten out their lives. He helped them get jobs and bank accounts and he tutored them to help them pass the GED."

"If he didn't cheat, what happened?"

"Some random psycho girl in the school fell in love with him. He never talked to her. He never coached her. He didn't even know her name. She had nothing to do with him and he never had anything to do with her. She just developed this fantasy life in her head where he loved her back and they were married with children and lived together in a house on Long Island."

"Jesus," he murmurs. "That's nuts."

"She really was. She got the idea that I was cheating with him and she came after me. She broke into our house and saw us together. We weren't doing anything except lying on the couch cuddling after work one day. She tried to shoot me and he jumped in front of me to protect me. She hit him instead and killed him. She went nuts when she realized he was dead and she tried to kill herself, but the Police stopped her. She's in a mental hospital upstate somewhere now."

He doesn't answer. I don't look to see his reaction. Maybe now he'll realize why I'm so wary of getting involved with someone in his situation.

Without warning, he slides his hand down the bridge railing and covers my hand with his. His palm radiates heat into mine and it rushes up my arm. He's touching me—like that.

This isn't a warm show of mutual sympathy and support. He means something else.

This is what he meant in the bar. He wants it to become more—but we can't.

Just then, a young woman jogs past us and disappears around the corner. Judah pulls his hand away and we lose contact with each other.

I turn in the other direction and keep walking. I don't know what's going to happen, but something is about to. I can't deny that anymore.

Judah walks next to me as big and strong and protective as ever. Now he knows as much about me as I know about him.

I don't pay too much attention to where we're going. Nothing *can* happen between us when we're out in public.

He surprises me out of my mind by grabbing my hand and pulling me sideways, off the sidewalk, into the trees.

He bursts through some bushes and I realize in an instant that no one can see us.

He pushes me against a tree trunk, but he doesn't squash his body into me. He just stands dangerously close so I feel the overpowering throb of his energy pulsing into me from inches away.

This goes so far beyond what I felt at the bar. He doesn't try to hold it back this time. He didn't try then, but now he just blasts it into me in all its volcanic power.

His nostrils flare and his eyes dip to my lips. I freeze in place when he slips his hand into my hair and bends down to kiss me.

His full, soft, strong lips take hold of me. The heat coming from his body melts the last trace of my resistance and I dissolve in that kiss.

This is nothing I haven't been fantasizing about for weeks, but it feels different in real life. His lips feel softer and yet stronger at the same time.

His tongue lights me on fire and I feel it traveling all over my body. It caresses me the way his voice does.

It threads between my legs the same way it snakes into my mouth. All that sizzling intensity makes him such a magnificent specimen of manhood.

He kisses me harder. I stretch on my tiptoes to keep up with him and that draws my body taut against him. His arms wrap around my waist....and then we fall back against the tree.

He still doesn't crush me under his weight. He lifts me a little higher so my body quivers with all this intoxicating passion washing through me.

His other hand closes on my breast and makes me squeal with a sudden rush of excruciating pleasure. My flesh throbs between my legs aching for him to touch me there.

He reads my mind, and without taking his lips away from mine, he guides my hand down between his legs.

I tense when I feel how thick and long and hard he is. His package spasms in my hand....and then he grabs me between my legs. I'm wearing pants this time and he massages and kneads and drives me wild with strong, deep squeezes.

I explode in screams as a bomb goes off inside me. I buck against his hand and convulse as a sudden, catastrophic orgasm hits me out of nowhere.

I forget to touch him back until he shoves his thick rod into my hand. I squeeze once and he reacts instantly.

He tightens his grip on my hair, attacks my mouth, and rubs me harder between my legs. I howl into his mouth, but he muffles the sound with masterful, punishing kisses. I can't escape the enthralling passion of that mouth.

I crash from one earth-shattering climax to another, but he never lets me go. He holds me there until I collapse against his chest. I have to tear away from his mouth and huddle there whining and sobbing as the last cruel spikes tear me apart.

He doesn't take his fingers out of my hair. He hugs my head against his jacket, and like something out of a dream, he rests his mouth against my hair. His warm breath spreads over my scalp.

I clamp my eyes shut. I can't touch him anymore. He draws his other hand out from between my legs and rubs my back instead.

It's such a comforting gesture and it means something more after what we just did.

I don't know how to cope with what just happened. I shouldn't have let it happen, but I wanted it to. I wanted it more than anything.

I don't know what it means or if it means anything. Nothing has changed for him. His life is still in pieces and I guess mine is, too.

He waits there until I relax enough for him to let go. He pulls his hands away and straightens up as if nothing happened at all.

He steps through the bushes and I lose sight of him. The rest of the world can see him. They can't see me until I step out there, too.

I find him waiting for me on the grass and we both head back to the duck pond. No one sees us. No one notices. No one is watching us.

They wouldn't see anything out of the ordinary if they did. We're both fully clothed and walking down the sidewalk side by side. Nothing to see here.

We head back to the bridge and stand there in silence. Will we ever say anything to each other again? Will we ever talk about what happened or will we both just go on as before—as lawyer and client?

I don't expect anything, but he surprises me again by covering my hand with his. "Thank you for telling me. It makes me feel better."

"I'm sorry for everything that's happening to you. I wish I could do something to make it better even though I know I can't."

"You are," he tells me. "Everything you are helps me. Just knowing you're out there in the world makes it better."

He squeezes my hand and we head back toward the oak trees. I don't know where this is going. It looks like it's going nowhere.

We stop on the street corner and he turns to look down at me. For some reason I can't understand, a beautiful, radiant smile spreads across his face.

I've never seen him smile like this before—not anywhere I could see him. He always holds it back or tries to.

He doesn't try to hide it now. He doesn't bite his lips to stop them from parting to show all his teeth. His eyes gleam with so much happiness it almost hurts to look at him.

"I guess I'll see you at our meeting on Monday," he murmurs.

I nod like an idiot. "Yeah. See you then."

His cheeks glow with light. I can't believe I'm looking at the same man. "Bye, Piper," he breathes.

I can barely choke out, "Bye," before he turns away and walks off up the sidewalk heading uptown.

Chapter 12: Judah

I stand on one side of The Billionaires' Club by myself. No one comes over to talk to me.

Kevin, Dante, Rory, and Jackson stride around the room, come together to consult with each other, nod, separate to different places, and then rejoin.

The rest of the members mill around talking and bullshitting and having a grand old time like they usually do.

This is the first time I've seen the whole membership in the club at one time. It looks like a lot more than thirty guys now that they're all in one place.

The noise in the room escalates to a steady throb of voices—or maybe I'm just more sensitive about the noise. My nerves can't take much more of this.

Dante finally raises his voice and yells over everyone else, "Okay! Listen up! This meeting will come to order."

"What are we here for?" Giovanni asks from the back. "Can't you guys run this club without consulting us? Isn't that why we have officers?"

"This meeting isn't about running the club—not that way," Dante replies and waves at Kevin.

He steps forward to address the members. This is it. It's hammer time.

"We called this special meeting of the whole membership because we have decided to expel three members from The Billionaires' Club."

A gasp rushes around the room. "Expel!" Saul Gottlieb blurts out. "You can't expel anyone—not unless their net worth falls below a billion dollars. That's the only grounds for expulsion—if someone no longer meets the entrance criteria."

"That would normally be the case, but we decided we had to make an exception this time," Kevin goes on. "These are extraordinary circumstances, so we decided we needed to take extraordinary measures to preserve the integrity of the club and continue to make it a safe place for everyone."

"Safe?" Niko Holloway chimes in. "What's not safe about it? It looks perfectly safe to me."

"I don't mean safe in the sense that someone might be in danger here—not physically," Kevin replies. "I mean safe in the sense that someone might endanger another member's reputation, their standing in the business world, and generally threaten another member's livelihood or some other crucial aspect of their life. That's what I mean."

A few more jaws hit the floor. "Who would do something as bad as that?" Diego Espinosa chokes. "We're all friends here—or we're supposed to be."

"That's what we thought, but these three members are obviously not our friends. They're here to prey on the rest of us, sabotage us behind our backs, and they're willing to use the club to do it. I'm convinced—and my fellow officers are convinced—that these members' actions have provided us with sufficient grounds to expel them. They won't be allowed back into the club. They won't be invited to any club functions. It's our hope as the officers of this club that none of our members will ever enter into any business arrangement with these men or give them any help, support, or assistance of any kind in the future."

More gasps and even a few yells drift out of the crowd. I never expected the members to react like this.

I guess someone getting booted out of The Billionaires' Club is a much bigger scandal than I realized. I didn't think the officers would go so far as to completely excommunicate the three offenders on top of everything else.

Cutting them off from doing business with the rest of us is a cruel blow. I didn't expect the officers to go as far as that. It really twists the knife.

None of the three offenders react right away. They don't know they got caught—not yet. They don't realize Kevin is talking about them.

The other members get the picture right away. "If you're going as far as that, you better tell us who these members are and what they did," Niko calls out. "We can't accept a punishment as harsh as that without some proof."

"We have proof," Jackson replies. "We aren't going to show it here on the club floor. That would be tactless and it would also be an insult to the injured party. You'll just have to trust that we've all seen it and it really is as damning as we say it is."

"What is it?" Niko asks again. "At least tell us that."

"Three members who are in this room right now knowingly went behind another member's back, had sexual relations with his wife on multiple occasions, and also brought her into the club and did it with her here on the premises. In some cases, they did it while members were in the club socializing with each other, and in some cases, they did it while the woman's husband was in the club socializing with the rest of us. We have security camera footage of them doing it. We don't need to show it. You'll just have to take our word for it."

Pierce Robbins and Tim Spader both glance over at me, but they don't say anything. Neither do I. I don't have to.

I should have expected the officers to preserve my anonymity. Lane doesn't say a word, either. He could tell everyone that I'm the injured party, but he doesn't. He protects me. They all do.

"We have decided to make an example of these three men so the rest of us can continue to belong to this club without the fear of them doing it to someone else," Dante goes on. "We're all supposed to be friends here. We're supposed to support each other and work together in ways we can't work with and get support from anyone else. These men threatened that. They could have destroyed it and driven out one of our most valuable members. We can't let that happen. We have to do the right thing by expelling these members so the rest of us can continue to uphold what this club stands for."

"If anyone here knows of another member who participated in this, we ask you to come forward with your information," Jackson announces. "If we find out later that anyone here knew of or protected anyone who participated in this, you'll be expelled, too. This is the only way we can preserve the integrity of the club and make it the haven it's supposed to be for all of us. We all need to be certain that our fellow club members aren't going behind our backs and hamstringing us from behind. We get enough of that from the outside world. We won't allow it here."

Dead silence falls over the group. No one moves until Giovanni asks in a shaky voice, "Who are these three members?"

"Peirce Robbins, Tim Spader, and Verner Smits," Dante announces.

Everyone turns around to confront the three offenders. Verner shuffles his feet and tries to avoid looking at anyone.

Pierce protests right away. "No, no, no! I never did anything like that! This is all bullshit! It's lies! Whoever came up with this is a liar!"

"Don't make us bring in the video evidence, man," Jackson snarls. "Do you really want us to show everyone here what a dirtbag you are?"

"I don't believe you have any video evidence," Pierce fires back. "I think you're making the whole thing up."

Kevin sighs and passes his hand across his eyes. "Come on, Pierce. You know you did it."

Pierce wheels around to face the crowd. "Which jackass here says I did it?! Which of you bitches has the nerve to spread lies about me? Come on! Face me, you pieces of shit!"

I bristle at those words. The cocksucker. I really hope the officers do show the video, but just then, Tim grabs his sleeve and tugs it.

Pierce whips around the other way like he wants to attack someone. He stops when he sees who it is.

Tim inclines his head toward the exit and jerks his head that way. Pierce frowns.

Tim nods toward the exit a little harder. Pierce shakes his head. What a buffoon.

Tim compresses his lips, takes hold of Pierce's arm, and hauls him out of the club by main force. Verner waits a few seconds longer.

Kevin waves him away. "I'm afraid I have to ask you to leave, Vern. Do us all a favor and don't ever come back here."

Verner tucks his chin and follows the other two out of the room. Kevin brings up the rear and leaves after them.

That leaves Jackson, Dante, and Rory standing in front of the shocked survivors. Rory doesn't say a single damn word through the whole meeting. He furrows his brow and keeps his mouth clamped shut in a deep scowl.

Dante finally sighs. "That's it. It's over. You can all go back to whatever you were doing. We're done here."

The other members murmur amongst themselves, and after a few minutes, Lane leaves followed by Giovanni.

Only one person looks in my direction. That's Niko Holloway. I can't tell from his expression if he understands that I'm the injured party in all this.

None of the officers come over to me. That would give it away. I meander through the room making my appearance and then I leave, too. It really is over. Now I just have to put the rest of my life back together somehow.

Chapter 13: Piper

I sit down at my desk and turn on my computer to check my appointments for the day.

I'm supposed to meet Judah at two o'clock this afternoon. Don't ask me how I'm going to deal with him after making out with him in the park.

Either way, we have things to discuss about his case, so I have to meet him. I'll just have to keep it professional.

He seems to want that, too, after the way he acted when it happened. He seemed to just want to walk away and move on. I can respect that.

He probably isn't ready to trust another woman. I can't blame him. He could stay single for a while after this divorce.

I frown at my schedule when I see a name at the top. *Mitchell Foster.* He's the most senior partner in our law firm, Foster, Carraway, and Barnett. Mitchell is basically my boss even though I'm a partner, too.

So why is he on my schedule for ten o'clock this morning? I would definitely know if I scheduled an appointment with him. I didn't.

I call my assistant. "Why is Mitchell Foster on my schedule for this morning?"

"He called an hour ago and asked you to meet him," she tells me.

"Did he say what it was about?"

"Nope. He just said he wanted to see you at ten o'clock today."

"That's weird. I wonder why he didn't tell me."

"Sorry I can't enlighten you. Do you want me to rearrange anything else? The meeting doesn't conflict with any of your other appointments."

"I guess not." I frown at the entry a little more and hang up. This is really strange.

It distracts me so much I don't get anything done for the next hour. I just have to wait to find out.

I go upstairs to Mitchell's office on the top floor of our building. I walk in and my blood runs cold when I find all the other partners there—all the senior partners.

"Take a seat, Piper," Mitchell tells me.

I drag my heels to the chair in front of his desk. The rest of the partners spread themselves around the room, but I'm obviously the specimen under the microscope here.

"What did you want to see me about?" I ask. I try to keep my voice steady, but I hear it shaking anyway.

"We know Judah Hayes engaged you to represent him in his divorce," Mitchell begins. "We also know about the accusation his former wife leveled against you that you were having an affair with him."

"It would be kinda hard for us not to find out," Carlton Swain adds from the side. "It's all over the internet."

"Nothing is going on between me and Judah," I tell them. "She's psycho. She just made it up to counter his accusation against her."

"We all know that," Mitchell replies. "We know you would never do anything like this. Unfortunately, we have no choice but to take you off Judah's case. Carlton and Shelby Tyson will take over for you and represent Judah from now on."

I cringe. I can just imagine Judah's reaction when he finds out. He's touchy enough about me knowing all his most closely guarded secrets. He won't be pleased when he finds out some strangers are going to go digging in his private business.

"This is in no way a punishment against you," Mitchell goes on. "You've always done excellent work."

"And no one here questions your integrity," Shelby chimes in. "We know you'd never cross the line with a client."

"So....you've already made your decision?" I ask.

"We have to," Mitchell replies. "Keeping you on as his lawyer only makes it look more like he's giving you preference for personal reasons."

I flinch at those words. I'm certain Judah is giving me preference for personal reasons—and not because he's attracted to me.

He trusts me. That's the bottom line. He trusts me with his money, his history, and his future. That's saying a lot.

I can't tell the partners that, though. That would only make it more obvious that *I* want to stay on Judah's case for personal reasons.

Mitchell apologizes a few more times and I make my escape. I don't care about anything else. I take the rest of the day off, text Judah to meet me at a café down the street from his office building, and leave work.

I get there half an hour early and pace up and down the sidewalk in nervous agitation. I dread this meeting, but I really want to see Judah. How did I get so attached to him so quickly?

I don't even know if I am attached to him. I care about him in ways I shouldn't if I'm going to be his lawyer, but I'm not his lawyer anymore.

He comes out of the building and frowns when he strides toward me. "What's so urgent? We were supposed to meet later today anyway."

"Come inside and sit down. We need to talk."

"That doesn't sound good."

"It isn't. Come on."

I lead the way inside and get a table near the front window. I don't have to worry anymore about anyone seeing us together. They can come to whatever conclusions they want about us.

Judah scowls even more when he sits down. "What's going on?"

I tell him about Mitchell's decision. "So Carlton Swain and Shelby Tyson will represent you from now on."

"I don't want another lawyer," he snaps. "I want you. I don't want some strangers going through all my documentation again."

"I understand, but they've already taken me off the case. I can't work on it now—not unless I quit the firm."

He tightens his lips. "I can't accept that."

"You can take it up with Mitchell, but you won't be able to change his mind. His hands are tied—and he's right. Me working on this case makes it look even more like there's something between us."

"But there isn't anything between us. I never cheated on Skyla with you." He bursts into a sudden grin as glowing as the one at the park. "I wanted to, but I didn't."

I feel my cheeks burning. "You didn't want to because you didn't know I existed until after you already split up with her."

"That's just a technicality. So....will you quit the firm to represent me?"

"I can't. I still have to make a living."

"I'll support you."

I snort. "Let's not start that."

I bend over to pick up my handbag. Now he knows. I can go back to the office now.

He stops me, cups my cheeks in both hands, and lifts my face to look deep into my eyes. "You aren't my lawyer anymore. You can go out with me now."

I want to brush that off with a joke, but the look in his eyes leaves me nowhere to hide. He really means it.

He has never looked at me like this—not ever. Some veil of reserve always stood between us. Now it's gone.

He leans in and kisses me—right in front of the window. "Come home with me tonight," he murmurs. "You can stay with me and....."

"Stop, Judah." I can barely husk those words, but I have to say them. "I'm not ready for that....and neither are you."

He stares at me with those bottomless eyes of his. What does he see when he looks at me like that?

He kisses me one more time, pulls away, takes out his phone, and does something on it.

"Don't be angry with me," I tell him. "We might not be lawyer and client anymore, but we still have obstacles in front of us—if we're even going to go there."

"I'm not angry with you—not at all." He sticks his phone in his pocket and looks up at me. "Do you need to go back to work now? Let me give you a ride."

I blink. "You're just....you're just going to drop it—just like that?"

"I'm not dropping anything. I want to go out with you. I want to be near you and talk to you and kiss you and put my hands all over you—but I understand that you aren't ready. I can take my time—and I can take my time until you think I'm ready. I'm in no rush here.'

"Are you sure about that?"

He splits in another incredible grin. Holy shit, where did all these grins come from?

Just then, a long, velvet-black limo pulls up to the curb outside. Judah takes my hand. "Come on. I'll drive you back to the office."

Chapter 14: Piper

I can't stop staring at Judah's limo on my way out of the café. Is he really going to give me a ride back to the office in *that?*

His driver opens the door for us. Judah holds my hand while I climb inside. Then he gets in after me and the driver shuts the door.

Judah slides across the seat and sits right next to me. He leans close to my ear and murmurs low in a satin undertone that shoots straight to my crotch.

"I want you," he breathes. "I've wanted you since the first day I met you. I want my hands all over you and inside you and holding you down. I want to feel you throbbing around me and taste you in my mouth. I won't stop wanting you just because you aren't ready. I can wait. Just know I'll take any part of you I can get. I want to take you out. I want to take you home. I want to strip you and dress you up and make you mine. I want all of you. I want to possess you. I want you in my life. I want everything you have and everything you are. I want to be the man in your life and in your bed....and I want you in my bed. I don't care how long I have to wait to get you because you're too good to pass up."

He barely gets the words out before he dives into my neck. His hot mouth closes under my ear.

I gasp as another rush of heat between my legs, and almost as if he knows, his dark, powerful hand closes on my thigh just below the hem of my skirt.

He crawls up between my legs, pushes them apart, and massages me through my panties.

I gasp and then start to moan. I don't have to hold myself back anymore. He isn't my client.

All the desire I've been hiding from him explodes off the charts. I've been hiding from myself, too. I've been hiding behind so many excuses about why I couldn't feel this way about a man again.

He gnaws down my neck, but my blouse and blazer stop him from getting any farther down. He spins around and plunges for my chest. He burrows between my breasts and tries to crawl down my shirt while his hand keeps drilling up my skirt and into my panties.

I heave on the seat trying to take him as deeply as I can. I want him to pull my panties aside and break me in half with his fingers. I want him to rip my blouse open and maul my breasts with his hot, greedy mouth.

Some distant part of my brain switches gears and I realize what I'm doing. I don't even know this guy. I held him at a distance all this time for a reason—and not because he was my client.

I can't do this. I at least have to find out more about him before I go there.

I summon all my effort to push him away. I shove against his shoulders to force him to sit up. Then I grab his wrist and pull his hand out from under my skirt.

It feels so trashy that I let him do this to me. I wanted it more than anything, but I can't do it like this.

I turn away from him feeling sick. I want him more than ever. Why can't I let myself have him?

I want everything he said he wanted to do to me. This inner barrier blocks me from what I most want.

I scoot farther down the seat to distance myself from him. The view out the window makes me want to cry.

This man sitting next to me right now—he's everything I want. I want him to trust me and lean on me the same way I trust him. So why can't I let myself lean on him?

He comes up behind me. I brace myself for him to start pawing at me and mauling me from behind. I should know better.

He wraps his arms around my waist, pulls me against him, and buries his face in my hair. He doesn't say anything. He just holds me there breathing into my scalp.

He doesn't say everything is going to be all right. I don't know if anything can ever be all right again. I don't see how it ever can.

If I don't find some way to love this man, maybe I'll never be able to love again. I might never find a man I love as much as this—a man who loves me as much as this.

Oh, what am I even thinking? I don't want to find another man. I want him. I need him. I need everything he says he wants to do with me. What is wrong with me?

He just holds me like that all the way back to my firm. The limo pulls up to the curb and the driver gets out. He doesn't open the door.

Judah unwinds his arms from around me. Now I can finally straighten out my clothes and try somehow some way to get myself in a condition to go back to work. How the hell am I supposed to do that?

"Will you be all right?" he asks under his breath.

I shrug at nothing. I'm not all right now. I don't want to be all right if I can't have him, but I don't say that out loud.

He raises his hand and caresses it down my cheek. He doesn't make me look at him or engage with him any other way.

He kisses the side of my head. "I'll be here waiting when you're ready," he murmurs.

"Don't you think....?" I don't know what I want to say.

I find myself looking up at him. He's my only refuge in this.....and I'm the scary monster I have to hide from. I'm the thing I need his protection from.

He cocks his head to study me. "What?"

"I thought....after what happened.....that you wouldn't be able to trust again." I look down at my hands in my lap. "Now I find out I'm the one who can't trust again."

"That's what I thought. I thought I would never be able to trust a woman again, but I trust you. I don't understand it. Maybe it's because you handle all my personal business in ways no one else does. You know everything there is to know about me and yet it's all right. I never worry about you judging me and I never worry about you telling anyone else." He looks away. "I guess that will all end now that I have another lawyer."

"Why me?" I ask.

"I don't know. I don't know what's different about you, but it is different. I don't care if the other lawyers see all my files and documents. I'll never trust them the way I trust you. It isn't the same. You just made me... you made me believe again. You made me believe there could still be good people out there—that there could still be a good woman out there. Your husband was a very lucky man. I understand now why he threw himself in front of a gun to protect you. I could see doing something like that for you. I couldn't see doing it for anyone else—but you? Definitely."

I have to look away. I want to hide in his eyes, but I can't. I can't stand the thought of someone feeling that way about me—not again.

What if something happens? What if Judah gets hurt because of me? What if I get hurt because of him? Too many things can go wrong.

I don't see Judah give any signal to the driver to open the door, but the driver does open the door. Maybe he just did it on his own initiative. I don't know.

Sunshine streams into the limo. It breaks the spell between me and Judah. "Come on," he murmurs. "You need to go back to work and so do I. We can see each other later."

He doesn't say when. He doesn't mention a time or a place when we might see each other later.

That could mean a lot of things. It could mean he doesn't want to push me too hard. It could mean he doesn't care enough to follow it up.

He cares enough. I don't have to ask about that.

He holds my hand to lift me out of the limo. He keeps holding my hand until I stand in front of him on the sidewalk. "Go to work," he murmurs low. "I'll still be here."

He gives me one warm, close kiss under my ear and pulls away. He turns me around so I face away from him and gives me a gentle push. I start walking and he vanishes behind me.

Chapter 15: Piper

I park my rental car in front of a nice red house on a leafy street somewhere in New Jersey. I peer through the windshield, but I don't see anybody.

Judah might get really mad that I'm here, but I have to find out the truth. I can't live with all his words ringing in my head—not until I know if he's sincere. I shouldn't let anything Skyla says influence me, but it does.

I get out of the car, take a deep breath, and walk up the driveway to the front porch. The front door stands open with the screen blocking the way into the front hall.

I ring the doorbell and hear voices yelling somewhere in the back. I can't tell if those voices belong to women or children.

Thunderous footsteps charge across the upstairs landing and a little boy barrels down the stairs. He skids to a halt in front of me, freezes on the spot, and scowls at me like I'm an alien from another planet.

"Hi," I begin. "I'm Piper. What's your name?"

He wheels away and tears into the back of the house at a dead run. He vanishes around a corner yelling, "MOM!!"

I shift my weight a few more times until a woman my age comes out of the back. She wipes her hands on a dish towel and scowls at me with an identical expression. "Can I help you?" she asks.

"Are you Jasmine Delvini?" I ask. "I'm a lawyer representing Judah Hayes in his divorce from his wife Skyla. I'm sure you heard the accusations she made that he had an affair with you."

She rolls her eyes, throws her dish towel onto a nearby chair, and gasps in exasperation. "Not that again!"

"He claims he never had more than one conversation with you and that his ex-wife concocted the whole story."

"She did concoct the whole story," Jasmine snaps. "He never gave me the time of day. He talked to me once at the company Christmas party. That's it. I never laid eyes on him again."

I nod. "He also claims you worked for the company as an independent contractor after you quit. Is that true?"

"Of course! What did you think—that he paid me off to keep me quiet about doing it with him?"

"Something like that, yeah."

She snorts. "Well, he didn't. That guy was as married as they come. He wouldn't look sideways at any woman other than his wife. It's a shame he got himself saddled with such a tramp."

I can't disagree with her there.

She narrows her eyes at me. "Are you really his lawyer? You aren't his girlfriend or something?"

"No, I'm not his girlfriend. I really am his lawyer. I just wondered if you'd be willing to testify on his behalf that you two never had anything more than a working relationship. It would mean coming up to New York. I'd ask you to fill out a deposition first. If that doesn't convince the court, then we'll need your testimony to squash Skyla's counterclaim."

"Absolutely. I would definitely come and testify if it meant finally putting this stupid story to rest. Nothing happened between me and Mr. Hayes. I barely even knew the guy."

Of everything she says, that last remark finally seals the deal for me. Mr. Hayes. She doesn't even call him Judah. She never could have had anything more than a professional relationship with him.

I thank her and drive back to New York. The drive gives me plenty of time to think.

Why did I even doubt that he was telling the truth about Jasmine? I didn't. I didn't doubt him. I doubt myself. Why?

Maybe I've just been stuck in this limbo of uncertainty for so long that I don't know how to snap myself out of it. I took myself off the market when my husband died.

I'm not on the market now, but it looks like I'm involved with Judah whether I want to be or not.

I shake that off. I can't be involved with him that way. I can't do anything with him half-assed. He wouldn't want that and neither do I

I do want to be involved with him. That's the thing. I want it real bad. So what's stopping me?

I drive back to the office and park in the underground garage before I go upstairs. I'm on my way to my office when Carlton Swain shows up.

"We'd like you to sit in on our first meeting with Judah Hayes, Piper," he tells me.

"What for? I'm not on his legal team anymore."

"You aren't one of the lawyers representing him, but you are an attorney with this law firm and you know more about his case than any of us do. We'd like you to be present in an advisory role. That's all. Besides, we think Judah would feel more at ease if you were there. He's more familiar with you."

I try not to snort in his face. Judah is definitely more familiar with me. He's a little too familiar with me.

I don't know if my presence will put him more at ease. It will probably just piss him off that someone else is representing him and I'm not.

That's Mitchell's problem, though, not mine. I finish what I'm doing in my office and get into the elevator to go upstairs for the meeting.

I wait for the elevator to get there. It stops two floors above mine. I stiffen when Judah gets into the elevator.

His eyes flash with danger when he steps inside. My presence definitely doesn't put him at ease. The tension spikes into the stratosphere. "Are you okay?" he asks in an undertone.

"Mitchell asked me to sit in on your first meeting with your new team—as an advisor."

"That's good," he replies. "I was hoping they would keep you involved somehow."

"I don't know how involved I'll be. This could be the only time I am involved. Even now, I don't know how much they'll actually let me participate. I guess we're about to find out."

He studies me for a minute with all his old intensity. What is he thinking?

He finally lowers his voice to a barely audible murmur and half-whispers, "Have dinner with me tonight."

My head snaps up. Why am I even surprised?

"We have no reason not to," he points out. "I promise nothing will happen. Just have dinner with me. What could possibly be wrong with that?"

"Besides confirming Skyla's accusation?"

He shrugs. "We wouldn't be confirming it. She still has no way to prove we were involved before the marriage ended."

He's right....and I really would like to have dinner with him. "All right," I agree. "I'll have dinner with you."

"Can I pick you up at eight? Give me your address."

I pull out my phone, but just then, the elevator door opens on the executive floor. I'm still in the act of emailing him my address when we cross the floor to Mitchell's office.

I can't help but see the irony. I'm at work and sending Judah my address so he can take me out to dinner tonight. We definitely aren't lawyer and client anymore.

We enter Mitchell's office to find him, Carlton, Shelby, and four other partners waiting for us. They all shake hands with Judah.

"We appreciate you accommodating this exceptional circumstance, Mr. Hayes," Mitchell begins. "I know you appreciate the work Piper is doing for you and that you wish to continue with her. This obviously isn't an ideal scenario, but we need to adjust based on the current outlook of the case."

"I'm only willing to accommodate it if the rest of your firm provides the same standard of representation I've come to expect from Piper. If I can't get that, then I'll have to look elsewhere."

"Of course. We all understand that." Mitchell waves to the chairs across his desk. "Please take a seat and let's get started."

Judah sits down. Every other seat in the room is already occupied by a partner more senior than I am. I have to stand.

I take a position off to one side where I'll keep out of the way. I'm prepared to go through this whole meeting without saying a word if that's what it takes.

Judah tightens his jaw. His whole expression goes dark and stony. I can't tell if anyone else in this room notices. I'm the only person here who really knows him.

Things go downhill the minute Mitchell opens his mouth about Judah's case.

"We're all familiar with the unfortunate publicity surrounding this case. We all understand the negative impact these things can have on a client's business—especially a business like yours that relies so heavily on clients trusting you with their investment dollars."

Judah stiffens in his chair and scowls even more ferociously. "What do you suggest?"

"The important thing is to settle this case as quickly as possible to minimize the damage. We just need to negotiate with the other party...."

"I won't settle," Judah snaps. "I made that clear from the beginning. I won't settle with her at all—not one penny."

"Unfortunately, the courts don't see it the way you do, Mr. Hayes," Carlton interjects. "The system is based on mutual..."

"Did you even read any of the documentation in this case?" Judah fires back. "Did any of you even read it? All my assets are protected by trusts and articles of incorporation. Skyla has no claim on any of that."

"The question isn't whether your financial position is protected enough...." Mitchell begins again.

"So you're saying I should let her blackmail me into giving her money?" Judah counters. "You're saying I should pay her off to shut her up to stop her from saying whatever she wants about me?"

"It's the quickest way to end the case and get her out of your life for good," Shelby replies. "It's the surest way to insulate your business from any further accusations...."

"What would stop her from making accusations in the future?" Judah demands. "I could settle the divorce and then she could write a book or go to the press and make up a bunch of other shit about me.

Then I would have settled for nothing. I won't settle with her. If you can't represent me on that basis, then you won't represent me."

"We don't need to turn this meeting into a conflict, Mr. Hayes....." Mitchell tells him.

"Apparently we do. Piper understood my position and she was prepared to represent me on that basis. If you aren't willing to do the same thing, then I have no choice but to seek representation elsewhere."

"There is the little problem of your former wife's counterclaim against you," Shelby points out. "Dragging all that through the courts would be the worst thing for your business and your reputation. It would be better to put the whole matter to rest now before it blows up in your face."

I can't listen to this anymore. "Actually, I visited Jasmine Delvini at her home over the weekend. She's adamant that nothing happened between her and Mr. Hayes. She's willing to fill out a deposition and even testify on his behalf if we need her to. She's as anxious to clear the air as Mr. Hayes is."

Everyone in the room spins around to stare at me, especially Judah. His eyes make me squirm. He's too smart not to realize the underlying meaning.

I drove down to New Jersey to investigate the infidelity accusation against him. I did that after Mitchell took me off this case.

I didn't question Jasmine Delvini as Judah's lawyer. I did it for myself—to find out for myself if he cheated on Skyla.

No one reacts to my announcement at first. Judah recovers first and waves at me. "You see? I'm in the strongest position here. Skyla has nothing on me. She doesn't have a leg to stand on when it comes to claiming any rights to my wealth. I won't compromise my integrity by paying her hush money to make her stop spinning these lies about me. That would be the worst thing I could do."

"Unfortunately, the law doesn't work that way, Mr. Hayes," Mitchell repeats. "Our policy as a firm...."

"I really don't care what your policy as a firm is." Judah stands up. His size casts an intimidating shadow over the other lawyers present. "You work for me. I pay you to represent me. I'm ordering you to pursue this case without settlement. The settlement option is off the table from now on. Is that clear?"

"Listen to reason, Mr. Hayes," Mitchell replies.

Judah casts one flinty glance over everyone in the room. He barely looks at me. "If you can't proceed on that basis, then we're finished here. I expect you to schedule another meeting where we discuss our real strategy—not this cowardly, backdoor diplomacy. I really expected better from your firm, Mr. Foster."

He walks out of the office leaving a chill behind him. The door shuts with an ominous click. No one moves for a second.

Mitchell finally signs and covers his eyes. "This is not good."

"What are we supposed to do if he doesn't settle?" Shelby asks. "What other option is there?"

"He can't seriously expect to take this to trial," Carlton exclaims. "He's out of his mind."

Mitchell turns to me. "What do you have to say about this, Piper? You know him better than all the rest of us combined. You can help us convince him."

"No one will ever convince him," I reply. "If you want my opinion, you should just plan to take it to trial. That's what he wants. He won't settle—not ever."

"There must be a way to make him see how misguided this is," Shelby points out.

"Why is it misguided?" I ask. "He has all his bases covered. He has no reason to settle except to compromise his own principles like he says."

"Did you actually encourage him in this hopeless strategy?" Mitchell counters. "I can't believe you would do something so counter to a client's interests."

"I didn't have to encourage him. He was adamant from our first meeting that he wouldn't settle."

"Still, a man in his position should be more discreet," Shelby remarks. "Doesn't he realize how much he stands to lose by letting this blow up all over the media the way he has?"

"Discreet how?" I ask. "All his assets are protected. I've never seen a client so well protected. From what I can tell, he stands to lose a lot more by settling than he would otherwise."

"That's a very irresponsible way to handle this case, Piper," Mitchell counters. "I'm shocked that you would mislead a client like this."

"I didn't mislead him. I followed his instructions which is exactly what you'll do if you represent him. He already understands the potential downside of this course of action. He can make his own decisions about how to handle this case. That isn't for you to decide on his behalf."

Mitchell gives me a dirty look. "I think we've heard your opinion enough for now, Piper. Thank you for your advice. You can go back to work. We'll handle Mr. Hayes's case from here."

I groan inwardly on my way out of the office. Fan flippin' tastic. These fools don't know who they're dealing with.

Judah will never compromise. He'll walk away from our firm if he thinks the senior partners won't pursue the case the way he wants them to.

Why the hell would he settle? He's holding all the cards.

Smearing his reputation with trumped-up accusations is Skyla's only weapon. If he doesn't cave, she has nothing.

I can't be the only person who sees that.

Chapter 16: Judah

I get out of the limo, walk up the steps of a tidy little brownstone on 73rd Street, and ring the doorbell. Is this Piper's house? She must be doing well for herself.

She's represented some big names. I'm not the only one who seeks her out for her experience and expertise.

I do my best not to shuffle my feet on the doorstep. Dating my ex-wife was never like this. I never had to stand on the doorstep and wait for her to answer the door.

Piper is so different from Skyla. Skyla never made it difficult for me at all. She was always delighted and waiting patiently every time I wanted to take her out. She always made it easy and effortless.

I have to be careful with Piper. She agreed to have dinner with me, but that doesn't mean anything. She could decide at any moment that she doesn't want to see me—not in that way.

Not being able to get her when I want her makes her irresistibly attractive. I have to have her. I have to win her somehow.

She's the first woman in my life I've ever had to win. I guess that's the real difference. Every other woman I've ever dated has just fallen into my arms with no effort at all.

Piper won't do that. Even making out with her doesn't make her mine. Making her mine will be a whole new challenge I can't even imagine yet.

She keeps her heart locked up behind a hundred iron walls. Her heart is better protected than my diamonds in the Antwerp vault. I can get them anytime I want them.

Her heart being out of reach only makes it more valuable. She's a priceless gem more priceless than any diamond. That makes up my mind for me. I have to win her. I can't pass her up.

She comes to the door wearing a little black dress that flares in ruffles at the bottom. She wears strappy black heels, but the rest of her is just as classy and understated as always.

She keeps the simple gold jewelry I always see her wearing at the office. She also leaves her hair combed straight down. She doesn't do it up to make it look fancier than it is.

Her simple beauty strikes me as so appealing that I get another stabbing wrench in the guts just from looking at her. She's beyond beautiful. She doesn't have to do herself up. She's perfect the way she is.

I want to put my arm around her and kiss her right here, but I said I'd take her out. I want more than her body. I want her to trust me enough to unlock all the doors to her heart.

She smiles up at me. "You look nice," she breathes.

"I'm sure I don't look as nice as you do."

She blushes and my arm just naturally migrates behind her back. My hand falls on her bare skin, but it feels natural to touch her like this.

I lead her down to the street and we get into the limo. The driver shuts the door and eases out into traffic.

I take another chance and slide my hand across the seat to take hers. She smiles at me. She doesn't hold back on that.

I find it difficult to remember that I made out with her at all. I could be going out with her for the first time. I *am* going out with her for the first time. This is the first time we've ever even spoken as anything other than lawyer and client.

I make a pact with myself right there not to talk about the divorce case or her firm or anything related to that. I'm not taking her out as a lawyer. I want to know who she really is underneath all that.

She squeezes my hand. Her fingers are too small for me to lace mine through hers. I just have to settle for holding her hand and feeling how small and delicate she is compared to me.

I struggle to come up with something to talk to her about. She saves me by doing it for me.

"Are you from New York?" she asks.

My head shoots up when I remember that she doesn't know anything about me.

"No, I'm from Illinois. I'm sorry. I should have told you more about all that."

She nods. "I thought you must be from somewhere in the Midwest. You don't have any recognizable accent."

"What about you?" I ask. "Where are you from originally?"

"Philadelphia. I moved here...." She trails off and doesn't finish.

"When did you move here?"

She squirms and looks away from me toward the window. "I moved here after college. I met my husband at Penn State and we moved here when he got a job at Bronx Community High School." She shakes her head. "Sorry. I shouldn't be talking about him."

"Why shouldn't you talk about him? He's your past. There's no need to deny it. It isn't like I don't already know."

"We should talk about the present instead."

I snort. "No, we shouldn't."

"If he's my past and I shouldn't deny it, then Skyla is your past and we shouldn't deny that, either. It isn't like I don't already know."

I want to look away, but I wind up turning to look down at her instead. Of course she knows. She knows everything.

I find myself smiling at her. "What is there left to talk about if we don't talk about your dead husband and my psycho ex-wife?"

She laughs. "The weather?"

"Why did you go into law?"

"My parents went through a nightmare divorce that ruined my father financially and my mother emotionally. I don't know why, but I got fascinated by the process. It happened when I was in middle school. I started reading up on divorce law when I was in high school—just to satisfy my curiosity about how it all went down. I just got really interested in it and I spent most of my high school years studying it on the side. I guess turning it into a profession was just the natural progression from there."

"Damn," I remark. "That is one hell of a story."

"Not really. What about you? What's your story?"

Right then, the driver pulls up in front of The Lighthouse Restaurant. I don't get a chance to answer before we go inside.

Piper cuts quite a figure on my arm. She glides with a grace and elegance I've never experienced with any woman. She makes me look so much better when I lead her inside.

I feel ten feet tall and bulletproof standing next to her. We wait for the concierge to come. Is everyone looking at us or does it just feel like that?

She floats up the stairs to the top floor where the concierge gives us a table in the very back corner. We're all alone here where no one can see or hear us.

I take her hand off the table, and just because it feels right, I kiss it before I hold it on the tablecloth.

She blushes, casts one sparkling glance around the restaurant, and settles into her chair. Her eyes glisten up at me with such depth. I could definitely get used to this.

"So you were going to tell me your story," she prompts.

"Oh, right." This gets easier with every passing minute. "Well, there isn't a lot to tell. I grew up in a working-class family and graduated from high school and everything the way most people do."

"How did you come to New York?"

"I had the brilliant idea that coming here would make me rich and famous."

She laughs. "Good idea. It worked."

I find myself laughing, too. She has that effect on me. "No, it didn't. I moved here, but the only job I could get was as a waiter in a café downtown. I stayed in a tiny windowless room at the YMCA. I couldn't afford anything else."

She leans forward drinking in every word. I can't remember anyone listening to me as intently as this—not for a long time.

"Anyway, after a year of that, I realized I wasn't going anywhere. I realized I would probably be doing the same job and living in the same room twenty years from now if I didn't change something—so I changed something."

"What did you do?"

"I got a job as a door-to-door salesman for a brick repair service. I had to go around to every brick building in the city and offer our services."

"And did you become rich and famous doing that?"

I laugh again. "Of course not. It was far more demoralizing than working as a waiter, but it did get me studying the sales process. I transferred to being a salesman for an investment firm and, for some reason, I did really well at that."

"Why do you think that is?"

"I don't know. Something about the investment world just clicked for me. I did well in their sales division and moved up. I started making more money and investing it.....and then a friend of mine suggested that we go into business together selling our own investment vehicles. It all kind of snowballed from there. We got an angel investor who believed in us and the whole enterprise took off."

"Who was the investor?"

I hesitate to drop a name from The Billionaires' Club, but she probably hasn't heard of it. No one has.

"It was Miles Reynolds. Don't even ask me what he saw in us. We had nothing going for us but enthusiasm."

"Maybe that's what he saw in you," she suggests. "Enthusiasm counts for a lot."

"You're right—and we knew how to sell. We sold him. I guess that's what made him stake us."

"That's an awesome story, too."

"I know it isn't as impressive as some. I didn't grow up in poverty or anything like that. The only obstacle I had to overcome was my own ignorance."

"That's a lot." She squeezes my hand. "It's impressive that you went from living at the Y to where you are now."

"I guess I'm still learning if I could get taken in by Skyla."

I shouldn't have said that when I'm sitting across the table from Piper. The words just slip out, but she doesn't react except to squeeze my hand again. "Do you want to talk about it?"

"I suppose we've already talked about it enough."

"What makes you think you got taken in by her? She told you she didn't care about money. It's understandable that you would be drawn to that."

I shrug that away. I just said I didn't want to talk about it, but I really do. I want to talk to Piper. I have to talk to her. She's the only person I can talk to about it.

"I don't think I was drawn to that at all. I mean, maybe I was on the surface, but not really. I wouldn't really have cared if she wanted jewelry or shoes or clothes or expensive trips or any of that."

"What was the appeal, then? Why did you pick her over all the other girls who wanted those things?"

"Probably because of her looks."

She gasps and her jaw drops. "Her looks! You were drawn to her looks?!"

"I know it's shallow. I was stupid—but yes. It flattered me that a woman so good-looking would turn her head for me. I suppose that's what took me in—thinking she could be attracted to an ogre like me."

Piper's breath stops. "You think you're an ogre?!"

"Well, I am. I'm a gargoyle."

She blinks at me in stupid disbelief. I can't tell what she might be thinking. Surely she can see I'm not chiseled out of marble.

I'm not a Greek god like Lane Prince or even a young stud like Giovanni Nowaczyk. I'm not good looking at all.

"What's wrong?" I ask. "Does it change your opinion of me that I would want a trophy like her?"

She shuts her mouth with difficulty and distracts herself by taking a drink from her water glass. "You are not a gargoyle, Judah," she murmurs.

"Well, I'm not a teenage heartthrob, either, am I?"

"Yes, you are!" she blurts out and immediately glances around to lower her voice. "Yes, you are."

Now it's my turn to pick my jaw up off the floor. "I am not! Are you insane?"

She gapes at me across the table. "You actually think that about yourself?! You actually think you're....you're ugly or something....or repulsive....or....." She falters as words fail her.

"I am ugly. I'm way too big and I'm...."

"For the love of God, don't say it's because you're black," she cuts in. "Please Dear God tell me you weren't about to say that."

"I wasn't going to say that." I find my face burning. How did this conversation go so wrong?

She swallows hard, leans across the table, and murmurs low in a barely audible undertone. "Listen to me, Judah. You are the best-looking man I have ever seen—bar none. You are gorgeous. You are a Michelangelo's David. Do you get it now?"

I gasp out loud. "I am not!"

She nods. "Yes. You are. Take my word for it. You're.....you're like some kind of god....or an angel or something. You look like a statue of something someone created as the most perfect specimen of humanity. Why or how a guy like you could ever find someone like me attractive is beyond comprehension."

"Are you out of your mind?" I have to fight my voice down. "You're stunning! You're beautiful—way more beautiful than Skyla."

She makes a face. "I am not."

"That's why I feel like an idiot for choosing her. She's fake. She's a doll. You're real."

I break off. I could say a lot of other things to try to convince her, but apparently this is what she's trying to tell me.

I can't believe she actually said those things about me. I can't believe it because it isn't true.

No one has to paint me a picture. I get to look at my own face every morning in the bathroom mirror. I know exactly what I look like. No one is pinning any medals on me for looks.

Then again, she must think the same thing about herself. She doesn't think she's good-looking.

Is it possible I'm as attractive to her as she is to me? I don't want to believe that. If it's true then we're both in this so far over our heads that neither of us will ever get out of it.

Chapter 17: Piper

J udah slides his hand across the restaurant table to take mine. He can do that, now that the server has taken our food away.

"So tell me more about your husband," he prompts.

"Why do you want to know about him?"

"I don't. I want to know about you. What was he like? I'm going to go out on a limb and guess that he wasn't a shallow, stuffed-animal-collecting streetwalker like Skyla."

I laugh. "No, he wasn't. He was just a guy with a big heart. He was very caring."

"I envy you for having that kind of relationship. It's something I can only aspire to."

I look away. I don't want to talk about my late husband, but I guess Judah is right and I'm just talking about myself here.

"Maybe we're in the same situation after all," I suggest.

He frowns. "How do you mean?"

"We're both trapped by the ghosts of a failed relationship."

"But you don't have a failed relationship. It wasn't a failure. You make it sound like it was a resounding success."

"But it's over now," I point out. "I'm just as single as you are. I'm not in that relationship and yet I'm trapped by it."

He leans a little closer and presses his fingers deeper into my hand. "You don't have to be."

"I don't want to be." I find it impossible to look at him. His eyes see too much. "I don't know how to break out of it."

He lifts my hand and kisses it again. "It makes me feel better that you want to."

"Of course I want to."

He sits back and gazes at me across the table. His eyes gleam with all their old fire, but the smile on his face makes him look so different. He looks so magnificently happy.

"I've been meaning to thank you for going down to Jersey and talking to Jasmine," he goes on.

I look away. "Don't thank me. My motives were purely selfish, believe me."

"I know. That's why I'm thanking you."

I look up at him. "What do you mean?"

"You're the only person in my life who actually takes the time to corroborate anything instead of just leaping to whatever conclusion they're going to leap to. No one ever checks out whether what I say is true or not. They all just decide whether they're going to believe it or not. It makes it impossible to know who to trust."

"How was I supposed to decide what to believe if I didn't check?"

He glances around the restaurant for no particular reason. "Can I ask you a question?"

"Of course. Anything."

"Do you think Mitchell, Carlton, Shelby, or any other partner in your firm ever actually read the documentation in my case?"

I blink at him, open my mouth, and stop myself. Did any of them read the documentation in his case? I can't be sure.

They could have gone through that entire meeting with him without having read it. None of them mentioned any of the details of his position.

None of them even seemed to be aware of the incredible measures he's taken to protect himself from a situation exactly like this one.

He snorts softly through his nostrils. "I thought so."

"That doesn't mean they haven't," I blurt out. "Just because....."

I trail off again. What am I supposed to say?

If they propose to represent his interests without reading any of the documentation, then they aren't doing their jobs as his attorneys, are they? They're neglecting their duties to their client.

I summon all my effort to go on. "I don't actually know if they have or they haven't read it. I wouldn't know because I'm not involved in the case anymore."

"But there's no question in my mind that *you've* read it," he goes on. "I know you have because we've talked about it. You didn't advise me until after you read it and clarified what you didn't understand. They're doing the opposite."

I squirm in my chair. "I don't think I should be talking about this with you. I still work for them. It isn't my business to criticize how they conduct a case that I'm no longer representing."

He doesn't get offended. He sits back in his seat, but he doesn't let go of my hand. He also doesn't stop looking happy. I don't understand why.

"Let's get out of here," he tells me. "It's time for me to take you home."

He leads me outside and his driver picks us up in the limo. Judah takes my hand as soon as we sit down on the seat.

That feeling that we're holding hands......that we're on a date.....I'm back on the market. I thought I would be off it for life. I didn't think I'd have to deal with any of this again.

I didn't think I'd have to deal with all these feelings again, either, but I am. Overwhelming feelings keep rushing through me. I don't know how to cope with them all or even how to identify which feelings I'm feeling.

Adrenaline pumps in my veins even though I'm just sitting here holding hands with Judah.

That on its own blows my mind. I'm holding hands with Judah Hayes, one of the richest men in New York or maybe even the country.

He looks straight ahead. He doesn't blast his powerful aura into me the way he did before. He really plans to just take me home, drop me off, and leave. He won't do anything. He promised not to.

I glance up at him—just for a second—and immediately look away. He doesn't notice until too late. He looks down at me, but I'm already turning to look in the other direction.

If I look into his eyes, I'll get lost in there. I don't trust myself, but I want to get lost in there. I want to get lost in the vast mystery that is him.

He doesn't do anything. He just sits there. He really won't because he said he wouldn't.

I need to. I ache to cross some line, to break something that can never be repaired. I need to do something to snap myself out of this mummified state.

I turn to look up at him. He barely glances at me. He isn't even thinking about that—but I am.

I throw caution to the wind and rotate all the way around in my seat to face him. I wind up kneeling on the seat next to him so I can look at him straight on.

Now I can admire his finely etched face, his powerful features, his bottomless, flinty eyes, and every grain of his smooth, flawless skin.

I raise my hand and stroke down his face from his forehead to his cheek. He darts his mouth sideways and kisses my hand.

I want to touch him all over. I can't do this from behind these fortifications of mine. I need to be the one to cross that divide.

I don't give myself an instant to decide one way or the other. I just have to do this. I need to drive a stake into the past and break from it. I'll die in the past if I don't do something now.

I lean in and kiss him. His lips melt in ways they never have before. They always overpowered me before—or tried to devour me in ravenous madness.

Now he just sits back on the limo seat and lets me kiss him the way I want to. I gaze at him and admire him while we kiss. I keep stroking my hand down his face. Every inch of his skin feels perfect and magical.

I kiss him a little deeper and turn my head to one side to open my mouth. His tongue meets mine.

That feeling of his tongue all over me starts to take hold again. I can't stop it. It threads between my legs and makes me bubble with juicy desire.

I struggle to breathe between kisses....and then his arms rise off the seat. His hands graze my sides through my dress. Does he feel how much I want him?

All the aching, torturous passion from the bar comes back with a vengeance. I was only kidding myself when I thought it wasn't there or that he wasn't feeling it anymore.

I lean deeper into him, but just then, the limo pulls up in front of my house. The driver doesn't get out. He stays in the seat without moving.

I sit back. Judah's features smolder with all that barely concealed volcanic heat. Even sitting this close to him burns my skin and he isn't even touching me.

His eyes search my deepest soul. He knows I want it. Why hide it?

I swallow hard, but I have to do this. "Would you like to come inside?" I whisper.

"I would love to come inside, but I don't want to do anything to pressure you or compromise you. If you have any doubts about this...."

"I don't," I blurt out. "I....I want you to....." My eyes float up to meet his. Just looking into his eyes like this makes me feel like I'm about to explode in rapture. "I need you to.....please."

He doesn't answer right away like he really needs to think about it. He drills me with such an intense, searching gaze that I can't keep still.

What if he says no? What if he decides that I'm not ready after all? I couldn't live with that.

He bends in and kisses me back, but it's the softest, gentlest, most caring kiss I've ever felt. I can barely hear him when he whispers, "I would be honored to come inside if you really want me to."

"I do," I husk.

He kisses me again and opens the door. He gets out of the limo first, takes my hand to help me out, and then sticks his hand through the driver's window.

I don't see what Judah does or gives the driver. They don't exchange any words before Judah follows me up the steps.

Chapter 18: Piper

My heart races when I unlock the front door and lead Judah into my house. He's only coming in for one thing.

Am I really doing this? Am I really bringing Judah Hayes inside my house? It doesn't seem possible, but it's happening.

Everything unfolds from somewhere outside me. I see myself doing all these things.

Inviting a man into my house is the last thing I would ever do—and yet I'm doing it. We just went out to dinner and now we're coming back to my house.

We're going to do it. This can't end any other way. That's why he's here—to break my dry spell.

This is more than that. This is way more than that because of the way I feel about him and the way he feels about me. I don't have to question that anymore because I know it's true.

He doesn't have to tell me how he feels about me. I see it in his eyes. I see it in the happiness radiating from his face.

I see it in the way he constantly bites back grins and laughter. He wouldn't do that otherwise.

I put my purse and keys on the table in the hall. "Come on in," I tell him. "Would you like a drink?"

"No, thank you. I don't drink."

"Would you like something non-alcoholic? I have iced tea, coffee, juices, milk....."

"No, thank you," he repeats. "I don't need anything to drink."

"Come in here." I lead the way into the living room.

I see myself going through all these casual little social graces. They don't mean a thing. They're the prelude to the main event—the real reason we're here.

I walk into the living room—and realize too late that I still have all the pictures of me and my late husband all over the room.

They line the shelf above the fireplace, the bookshelves, and the side table. They show us hugging, laughing, smiling, and even one with him kissing the side of my face.

Judah strolls past them looking at each one before he sits down on the couch. His sharp eyes trail over the rest of the living room. "This is nice. You have a very nice house."

"It isn't as big as yours...."

"That's why it's nice. It's more comfortable. Mine is a trophy like everything else in my life."

I turn bright red. "I just realized right at the moment when I invited you in here.....This is the house I lived in with him. We lived here together. That's why it looks like this." I wave at the pictures. "I guess it was massively inappropriate for me to invite you here."

"Not at all. I like it." He looks straight at the pictures.

"You do? You don't feel.....?" I don't say it.

Maybe he feels creeped out by sitting here with me while my dead husband watches us from those pictures. This must be how Judah felt trying to sleep with all Skyla's stuffed animals watching him.

He reads my mind. "No," he murmurs. "It doesn't bother me at all." He turns to face me.

Those eyes wipe out everything else, including the pictures of my dead husband.

In fact, Judah's eyes *don't* wipe out the pictures of my dead husband. Judah wants my dead husband to see.

Judah wants my dead husband to see me coming back to life with a living, breathing, strong, caring, vibrant man. Of course my dead husband would want me to do that.

Reading that truth in Judah's eyes tears down the last barrier. I want this. I want this more than anything and now nothing stands between me and Judah. If anything, this moment makes it possible.

I swivel around on the couch to kiss him the way I did in the limo, but the charge shooting back and forth between us makes this lightyears different.

He raises his hands right away and doesn't hold back. He strokes them down my sides, behind my back, up to my hair, and down to my hips.

I escalate much faster this time. The fact that my dead husband is watching me skyrockets my desire off the charts. I'm doing it with Judah—or I'm about to.

The dam breaks and unleashes all the restrained passion I've been hiding from him all these weeks. I didn't want to admit even to myself that I wanted him this much—that he could affect me this much.

I lean into that kiss. Both our heads tilt sideways and our mouths open to meet each other.

His tongue slithers around mine and all his magnetic heat floods me to the breaking point. I pant to keep up with him. My body won't stop trembling with all this insatiable need for him.

He won't take it any further, though—not without me inviting him to. I climb onto his lap and straddle him.

I feel the iron hardness of his shaft inside his pants. That feeling, the throbbing length I felt in the park—it blows my mind apart. I have to feel him. I have to take him all the way in. I can't let tonight end without that.

I crush myself down on him and reel in the torturous spasm of his muscles contracting between my legs. I need more of this. I need it all to tear me apart and leave me in pieces so I can put myself back together.

Judah matches my rhythm exactly. His hot, strong hands circle my waist. His fingers dig into my hips to tug my skirt up.

The sensation of the fabric slipping over my thighs turns me on like nothing else. I whimper in his mouth and then he darts his hands under my dress.

His fingers scorch my skin crawling around to my panties and my ass. He grips my thighs inching higher toward the crease where my legs join my hips.

I can't stop riding on his lap while we kiss. His breath blasts into my nostrils from his nose. His mouth tastes intoxicating and heavenly.

I need to touch him, but I can't do that with his clothes in the way. I slip my hands under his jacket and feel his muscles strain inside his shirt. I want to touch all of that. I want to see how beautiful and strong he is underneath this polished exterior.

Before I can think to start working on his shirt buttons, he closes both arms around me—one behind my neck and one behind my back.

He pulls me against him and rocks in a blissful, heartfelt embrace of deep emotion. My body keeps riding him and he keeps pushing me down on that spiked tool between his legs, but this means so much more.

He cradles me with such tenderness that I can't stand it. I whimper in rapture just from being in his arms. I hug him around his chest with all this feeling bursting out of me.

I don't even care anymore if I do it with him as long as I can feel this—just being with him.

He means so much to me. How did that happen? How did it happen that I care so much about what happens to him?

I want everything to work out for him. I want him to heal from his divorce the way I need to heal from my husband's death. I want to be that person for him the same way he is for me.

He pushes me up and the light coming from his eyes captivates me in another tempest of emotion. This is deeper than sex, deeper than attraction, deeper than respect.

He leans forward and yanks off his jacket before he settles back on the couch. His white shirt looks somehow even brighter against the dark skin of his neck and hands.

I caress over that white expanse feeling his energy pulse through the body underneath. He's just as hypnotically alluring under there as he appears from the outside.

He copies me by trailing his hands all over my body. He tiptoes his fingers over my dress nudging it higher....and then he lifts it over my head.

He lets it fall and moves toward my neck with his mouth open.

I explode in hoarse, choked screams when he bites into my neck. His hot, blistering mouth crawls lower toward my cleavage. I can't stand this.

That blast of energy shoots down my stomach to my quivering flesh. I grind harder on his package and he responds by escalating to match me.

He seizes me with both hands, crams me down on his lap, and mauls my chest down to my bra cups, but he doesn't try to remove them.

He inhales deep, ravenous bites through the cups to make me scream. I feel myself spiraling out of control.

I try to distract myself by tearing at his shirt buttons, but he doesn't make it easy when he's burying his face between my breasts.

I clasp his head against me in between ripping his shirt up and trying to flick open his buttons. He lets go of me for two seconds to help me get his shirt open before he attacks me with both hands again.

He tears off, straightens up, and the volcanic look in his eyes makes my head swim. He glares at me in primal madness. The pulse of hot blood between his legs cascades through me with a beat like the waves of climax sweeping me away.

He locks those eyes on me, and like a dream, his hands take over my whole world. He snakes his fingers into my hair, tightens into an unbreakable grip, and his other hand drills between my legs.

In a split second, he penetrates inside my panties and all the way in.

I want to scream again, but the shock and thickness of his fingers makes me gasp instead. I stare. I barely see him in front of me....and then I do see him.

One hand grips me by the hair and the other drives in deep. That sensation of him splitting me in half blasts me into the stratosphere.

I teeter on the brink of insanity and then a colossal explosion detonates out of me.

I shriek once before he pulls my mouth against his to muffle the sound. I can't kiss him. I'm climaxing too hard on those fingers. They milk every drop of rapture and ecstasy from my deepest being.

My husband is seeing me like this. He's seeing me fall apart for another man.

It's okay because it's Judah. He's the one doing this to me. He has me. He's taking me the way he wanted to in the bar. Circumstance got in the way, but he never stopped wanting me.

I thrash in his grip, but he doesn't let go. His arm strains under his shirt. My hand lands on his bicep and I feel him pumping deep into me to give me all this mind-blowing pleasure.

He growls into my mouth and uses his grip on my hair to push me down harder onto his hand. I crumble in an earth-shattering climax. Brutal screams rip from my soul, but only he hears me. Only he knows how he's bringing me to my knees.

I surrender to that unbreakable hold. I don't want to escape. I want him to take over so I don't have to. Will he take me? When will he take me and how?

I can't stop slamming down on his fingers, but before I even finish convulsing in the throes of passion, he tips me back.

He has to untangle his fingers from my hair before he sits me up straight. His fingers glide all slippery and wet from between my legs.

I have a hard time focusing my eyes on his. I sense that intoxicating look holding me in his power, but my vision keeps drifting in and out of focus.

He kisses me once, murmurs under his breath in animal satisfaction, unclips my bra.

I expect him to attack my chest again, but he doesn't. He wraps his arms around me, lifts my weight off his lap, and lies me on the coffee table on my back.

I sprawl in front of him still drunk with the waves of bliss pulsing through me. I don't know what's happening until he slides my panties down, spreads my thighs, and lowers his face to my dripping slit.

I gasp again as the first delicious flick of his tongue detonates my mind. I quiver all over, but he doesn't escalate.

He holds my thighs apart and delivers one soft, sensitive, brutally cruel lick after another. He keeps his touch so light and fairy soft that I can't stand it.

I sob and moan on the table trying to buck against his face, but he holds me down in that position.

I feel myself careening away into some other dimension—a dimension alive with pleasure and mind-numbing ecstasy. I might already be there. In fact, I know I am.

He uses the very smallest tip of his tongue to circle my clit and tease me to the brink of destruction. I need so much more.

The strength and command of his hands holding my legs down electrifies me like nothing else. I can hurl myself against that hold and fly all the way out of my mind. I'm safe in his hands. I don't have to control myself anymore. He's doing it for me.

I try to touch his head. His skull and scalp seem so much hotter like this—with his face buried between my legs and my flesh spread out for his delight.

He alternates between little delicate flicks of his tongue to soft, deep, warm, wet licks that melt me in his hands. Every lick brings a gush of pleasure from my swollen channel.

I want him to get up on his knees and drive into me. I want to lie here while he takes me. I want him to see me succumbing to all this drunken madness of desire for him. I want him to conquer this body and make it his own for all time.

I arch my head back and I really do scream as the next ebb of climax takes me. His hands migrate up my body to clasp my breasts in powerful squeezes.

He finches and fondles my nipples, but those sensations get swallowed by the massive breaking wave of torrential passion consuming me right now.

Chapter 19: Judah

I can't get enough of Piper lying spread-eagled on the coffee table in front of me. I don't ever want this to end, but it has to end sometime.

The way she's giving herself to me—I never could have imagined this in my wildest dreams.

She's so magnificently beautiful. She's even more beautiful for the emotion she puts into this.

I've never experienced a woman giving me her heart like this before. I thought other women did, but I was wrong. This is the real deal.

I have to look at her. I'd like to spend the rest of my life with my face buried between her legs, but the sight of her arching her back and thrusting her breasts into my hands proves too tempting.

I straighten up, and when I do, I just have to hold her. I scoop her up and pull her back onto the couch. She winds up straddling my lap the way she did before.

I expect her to cycle down and fade off, now that she's had her climaxes. I can live with that. I can give her this one night of pleasure and go home by myself.

Just feeling her, kissing her, tasting her, fingering her, hearing her screams and moans—all those sensations make tonight a success. I don't need anything more than that.

She collapses on my shoulder whimpering and sobbing. Her body quakes with spasms.

She feels so impossibly good in my arms. I can't stop kissing her hair and ears and neck and the side of her face. I don't need to kiss her on the lips.

Okay, I do need to kiss her on the lips, but not now. Her lips will always be mine to kiss. I know that now. I'm the only man taking her there.

She gives herself to me so beautifully. I can't wait for next time. Just the sound of her sobbing and moaning in my ear gives me superhuman strength.

I pet her hair and run my hand down her back to help her power down. She probably wants to crawl into bed and pass out now.

I love that I'm the one who gave her that. I love that I made her scream and contort and thrash with pleasure. Mmmm. She's beyond sweet.

I'm just about to say good night to her when something changes. She doesn't take her head off my shoulder. Her hair spills over her face. Her body flops against me in limp exhaustion.....and then she raises her hands to the buttons of my shirt.

I stiffen when she starts unbuttoning them. That feeling of her undressing me.....it sends another shiver through me.

Her breath catches and then strains as she crawls her mouth up to my neck. She takes one moist, succulent bite of my neck and drags her torturous burning lips down to my collar.

She unbuttons my shirt one excruciating button at a time while she migrates lower toward my chest. She pushes my shirt open and then she's on me.

I hiss between my teeth at the sensation of her lips leaving those brutal kisses all over me. She slides her tongue down my sternum and then mouths sideways to each of my nipples.

I freeze at the first bite. She barely nicks my nipple with her teeth before she's gone. That lightning bolt of sensation shoots straight to my nuts. My shaft aches from the pressure.

She reads my mind, and before I can even move, she shoves her hand between my legs and starts rubbing me to death. I flinch and then an earth-shattering wave of pleasure rushes through me from her hand.

She strokes me through my pants burrowing lower....and lower.....

She shoves my shirt all the way open to expose my chest and stomach. Her delicate little hands look so white against my skin.

Those hands burn trails of fire through me. She won't stop touching me even as she tugs my belt open. Her hands hold me spellbound running across my chest, around my ribs, under my arms, over my shoulders, up my neck, and trail across my lips.

I stare down at the top of her head when she buries her face in my crotch the same way I buried mine in hers. Is she really doing this? Is she really going there?

I don't even have to ask. She yanks my belt open and nudges my pants and underwear down until I sit up enough for her to pull them off.

She slides them down past my knees and then her cruel, strong mouth takes hold of me. I groan in ecstasy as her tongue circles my shaft. Her sizzling, magical saliva coats me and her strong tongue takes me all the way in.

Her magnificent body undulates in front of me in time to her rhythm. I want to touch her. I want to follow every blissful curve of her taking me, but I can't interfere with this. I can't do anything to interrupt this mind-blowing fantasy coming true.

Her hazy eyes float up to meet mine. My prick spasms from the look in her eyes. Her mouth slides down my shaft and her sucks wring every ounce of my resistance from me.

She closes her eyes and falls on me with new enthusiasm. She bends over me and I catch a glimpse of her sweeping curved waist running all the way down to her perfect ass.

I collapse back on the couch gasping for breath. I can't take much more of this.

I grasp at her shoulder to pull her off, but I can't even do that. I can't do anything with these crushing sensations wiping me out.

Without warning, she takes hold of my hand and moves it to her head. She places my hand on her head and her rhythm changes.

That feeling of her head moving up and down under my touch feels so incredibly hot that I can't stand it. I teeter closer to the breaking point, but right then, she slides off and climbs back onto my lap.

Now she's completely naked. She doesn't let go of me. She straddles my lap and guides me inside her.....where I belong.

I want to collapse right now, but the only place left to collapse is right into her arms. My face falls into her breasts. My arms circle her waist and then we're moving together in a rhythm that never ends.

She whines higher, holds my head against her breasts, and her hot mouth falls against my ear. She moans and sobs straight into my brain.

That sound tightens a stranglehold on my nuts and I pump into her faster. I need her too much. I need every inch of her channel clenching around me.

She grinds faster cycling up to another climax. Her fingers dig into my scalp and then my neck, back, and shoulders. She claws at me trying to hold it all together even though it's way too late for that.

I could just sit here and let her ride me, but I want more. I take hold of her and scoot to the edge of the couch where I can control her movements better.

I keep my arms strapped around her waist and thrust up into her from below. She bumps off my hips and her thighs slap me with each beat.

She shrieks each time I drill into her. I love that sound, but her mouth attracts me with an irresistible pull.

I lift my head to kiss her....and then I get lost in the heavenly velvet of her mouth consuming my mind. Her undulations match my rhythm exactly. Our bodies beat together like we were made for this—because we were.

I pull her in with each stroke. Then, when I relax, she falls off so I can thump into her again.

Her channel coats me with slippery goodness. She shudders and sobs when I pull out, only to scream in mystical ecstasy when I corkscrew in for another thrust.

She breaks off my mouth and her head lolls back. Her face dissolves in an angelic glow of rapture. The light coming from her half-closed eyes and flushed cheeks—she makes me almost want to cry when she looks like this.

I try to hold her close, but I wind up tightening my grip on her. My body won't last much longer. She feels too good. The deep, heart connection between us carries me higher.

She doesn't notice—or maybe she does. The faster I go, the deeper I strike, the faster she hurls herself down on me. She gallops faster to encourage me to take her.

I try to kiss her, but her lips don't respond anymore. She yelps at each thrust and then she buckles on my shoulder screaming, sobbing, and thrashing in my arms.

The spasms of her inner muscles as she reaches another epic climax flood down my shaft. They stroke me faster and deeper.....and I erupt into her. I crush her in my arms.

Her blissful sobs stab me in the brain. Her sweet honey pours over me, but the ecstasy of wrapping my arms around her and cradling her in this warmth overpowers everything else.

Chapter 20: Piper

I come to my senses sitting sideways on Judah's lap on the couch in my living room. I can't remember how I got into this position, but it doesn't matter.

He has his pants pulled up, zipped, and buttoned, but he isn't wearing a shirt.

The heat coming from his massive chest and arms keeps me warm. I would be cold otherwise. I huddle closer to him and he kisses me on the forehead. Did I pass out after that last climax? I must have.

I'm still dazed and barely conscious when he whispers down into my hair, "It's all right, baby. You're safe. I'm here. Nothing will happen to you."

I can't keep my eyes open. I can't remember ever feeling this exhausted.

I curl into a ball on his lap and he picks me up in his arms. I knew he was jacked under his suit. I just never imagined he would be this jacked.

He carries me easily in a baby cradle hold with my head resting on his shoulder. I wrap my arms around his neck and cling to him. I need protection from this sensitive, fragile feeling. I've never felt this sensitive after sex.

I can't even call what we did sex. It was something so much more than that.

He carries me out of the living room, switches off the light, and climbs the stairs. He pauses at each bedroom door to look in before he comes to the master bedroom.

He doesn't show any sign that the pictures of my late husband bother him here, either. Judah sits down on the bed, pulls down the covers, and then lowers me into them.

I hold onto his neck at all costs. "Don't leave, Judah," I croak. "I need you here."

"You need to sleep, baby," he murmurs and kisses me on the forehead again.

"Let me sleep with you." I'm getting emotional from all the crazy energy going through me. I still feel shaky and vulnerable from doing it with him. "Please....stay."

He sighs and sits down on the bed next to me. He tucks the covers over me. I can't stand that. I can't stand the feeling that I'm in this bed alone without him.

Before I know what's happening, I turn my face into the pillow and burst into tears. I don't want him to think I regret doing it with him. I don't. I just want him here. I want him in this bed with me.

"It's all right," he breathes. "It's all right. It's okay."

"You said you wanted.....to be the man.....in my life.....and in my bed...." I wail. "You said......you wanted.....that,,,,,,"

"I do, baby," he whispers. "I want that more than anything."

"Please stay!" I howl. "I need you here! Don't leave."

He compresses his lips. "You said you weren't ready. Do you remember that?"

"That was before! I need you now!"

I can't face this. I don't know why I feel so devastated by the idea of him leaving. I only know I need him. I can't face this without him—without feeling that he's here for me.

I crossed a divide to get together with him. Now I don't know what's happening to me.

He comes to some decision, pulls his pants off, and crawls into bed next to me. He pulls me over onto his chest.

That feeling of him holding me makes me break down crying even harder—with relief this time. He's here. I'm okay because he's here.

I can be as fragile as I need to be as long as his arms protect me....from myself. I need protection from myself—from this feeling that my life is coming apart at the seams.

The sobs keep pouring out of me for a long time. I don't know where all this is coming from, but I feel better, now that I can finally let it out.

I get tears all over his chest, but he doesn't seem to care. I finally use the sheet to wipe them away and grab a tissue from the nightstand to blow my nose.

He adjusts his arms each time I need to move. He doesn't stop me from doing anything or try to comfort me in any other way. He just lies there holding me until I stop crying.

I crawl back into his arms and he folds his warmth around me exactly the same way. He feels even bigger like this.

I finally work up the courage to whisper out my worst fears. "What's going to happen to us?"

"I don't know," he murmurs back. "I've never done anything like this before. We're in uncharted territory."

I hesitate and then ask, "Is this what you wanted? Is this what you said you wanted?"

"This is what I said I wanted, but I didn't know it would be like this. I don't know what I thought, but like I said, I don't recognize this. I've never experienced anything like this before."

I don't know how to answer. I've never experienced anything like this, either. I've never been with a man like Judah before.

I tilt my head back to look up at him. His dark face looks ghostly in the shadows. Faint light from outside the window gleams on his forehead and eyebrows.

It casts a silver line down his cheekbone to his jaw and lips. He lies with his eyes closed.

I don't know what I expected from this, either. Never in a million years would I have expected it to turn out like this. I don't even know what this is.

Doing it with Judah downstairs and now lying in bed with him—it seems so.....so casual, but it isn't. It's much more than that.

I want to ask again what's going to happen between us and whether this is what he wants. Does he still want it after I fell apart just now?

He probably wants to leave. That must be why he brought me up here. He planned to put me to bed and then go home to his own house. He wasn't planning to spend the night.

I'm not sure I want him to spend the night. I should be taking this more slowly.

I cringe when I see pictures of my husband all over the room. Judah is right. I'm not ready for a relationship. I'm obviously holding onto my husband and our past too much to move on.

I'm not ready to take those pictures down, though. I don't want to move out of this house even though this is the house where my husband died.

I don't want to move out of this house *because* it's the house where my husband died. God, how pathetic does that sound! I'm like a zombie living in a mausoleum. I'm a skeleton mummified in a past that no longer exists.

I really need to change that. Doing it with Judah doesn't change it. I need to do something else, but I can't think what that would be.

"Why do you like diamonds?" I ask.

The words come out before I even think about them. They surprise me. I don't know why I even ask. It isn't my business.

He jumps a little bit like the question surprises him, too. Maybe he thought I was falling asleep.

"Hmm? I like them because they're pure and beautiful—and because they're a good investment."

I snort with sudden laughter. I feel lighter after all that crying. "Is it always an investment with you?"

He grins and the silver line on his face changes shape. His eyes drift open and catch the light. It reflects off his teeth. He looks happy again. "Apparently it is."

"How did you get into it?"

"Miles Reynolds was an avid stamp and coin collector. He used to yack our ears off for hours about his collection whenever we went to his house—and anytime we met him in any public setting. He was a freak for his stamps and coins. It was like pulling teeth to get him to stop talking about his collection and concentrate on business."

He laughs. He sounds so different now.

"Then I met another billionaire with an exotic car collection. I guess I started thinking I needed to collect something—or at least have an interest outside of business. I did some research on all the things people collect. I found out people collect things like vintage barbed wire and rail spikes, die-cast, toys, furniture, antique typewriters, musical instruments, tennis rackets.....I thought, that is all way too bulky. I need something that won't take up any space. Then I found out about diamonds and precious stones and it all went downhill from t here."

He laughs again and his eyes glow.

"I don't know why I do it. Maybe it's the feeling that I really am as rich as everyone says I am. The diamonds are the most tangible proof of that."

"But you own all those real estate investments," I point out. "Aren't they tangible enough for you—and they're a lot bulkier."

He laughs even harder. The sound comes from deep inside his chest.

"You're right, but I don't have to store them in my house." He turns to me. "What about you? Do you have a hobby?"

"Not really. I guess I'm boring that way."

He turns his head just a little more to face me. "You definitely aren't boring."

The look in his eyes sends a shiver through me. He bends a little closer to kiss me and then his weight covers me as he rolls on top of me.

The energy escalates much faster and much hotter this time. He doesn't sit back waiting for me to initiate.

He kisses me fast. I have to work hard to keep up with him, but the torrential passion of those kisses catapults me into another dizzy spiral. I'm going there with him even faster and harder this time.

He burrows his hips between my legs and I wrap myself around him to take him in. I want to feel how thick and hard and strong he is. I want him to devastate me with his power and he doesn't disappoint m e.

He arches up on his thick, muscular arms. His whole body contracts with muscle as he pumps into me.

His thrusts shatter me in delirious waves of bliss. I can't even scream as the explosion hits.

I stare up at him glaring down at me with those brutal, masterful eyes. He hypnotizes me into a sex-fueled trance. The ecstasy pulsing through me shimmers in my eyes and mesmerizes me under his spell.

I could lie here until the end of time and let him see me totally exposed to him. His eyes trace down my body to my breasts and stomach and spread thighs.

He drinks in every sight and sensation. His lips shiver off his powerful teeth as his own passion builds to the breaking point.

I expect him to explode into me, but instead, he eases back on his knees, grabs one of my legs under my knee, and pushes my leg farther up.

That angle stretches me just a little more and makes me even more sensitive to how thick and veiny his shaft feels. My head rolls back and my vision blurs as I moan in torrential agony.

He growls at me through his teeth. That sound conjures up so many feelings of animal madness taking hold and carrying both of us to another world. Humanity slips away and we become nothing but cosmic beings coming together in the primal mists of time.

I release all the forgotten instincts hidden in my body. Pure instinctive carnal hunger for him takes over. His lips curl back in a feral snarl.

I try to touch him, but he's already too far gone. He shoves my leg higher and leans over to drive me into the bed.

He shifts his weight just a little more to the side. His arms close around me in a crushing hold. I can't get away from the electric shocks he keeps delivering to my deepest core.

I don't want to get away. I want him to pulverize me harder until I collapse into him forever and always.

He lowers his husky, hot mouth to my ear and pounds in extra hard. His voice rasps in wordless animal snarls as his shaft strains to the breaking point.

I hear myself whining for it, but I want that. I want to be shameless and abandon all connection to everything that once held me back.

He seems to understand that I need this. He drills in extra hard like he needs to break me apart—because he does. I need him to shatter this hard outer shell protecting me. Then nothing will remain but the soft inner heart that belongs to him.

Chapter 21: Judah

I sit up on the edge of Piper's bed and look down at my hands. They don't seem to belong to me anymore.

Spending the night changed me. I just don't know how yet.

She scoots over in bed and runs her hand down my back, up to my neck, and strokes my head. She seems particularly attracted to my head. She's always caressing it and kissing it and breathing on it.

I shiver when I think about last night. I told the truth when I said I've never experienced anything like this.

I've never met a woman who exposes her heart and soul so purely and so openly. She lets me look straight into her precious heart while I take her.

Would I have come this far if I'd known it would be like this?

I probably wouldn't have. The way I feel about her scares me. It scares me because she trusts me so much.

It isn't even about me trusting her because I do. She can ask me about my diamonds and I don't have to lie or worry that she's going to use the information against me.

It's the way she trusts me that makes me tremble. She places her most fragile being in my hands. I could wreck her if I wanted to, but I don't want to.

I want to protect her. I have to be extra careful that I don't hurt her.

I could never hurt her. I know that now. I would give my life for her. I would do a hell of a lot more than throw myself in front of a gun for her.

The sight of so many pictures of her dead husband reinforces the massive responsibility I signed myself up for. He's watching me. He's checking to make sure I treat her right.

I have to step up my game big time if I want to get involved with this woman. I can't go playing house the way I did with Skyla.

This is serious business. This is beyond serious. This is life and death.

I've been telling myself since long before I met Skyla that I wanted children. I set up my trust for my future children.

I never talked to Skyla about having children with her, though. How interesting. It never once crossed my mind to go there with her.

I told myself I wasn't ready. I told myself I would do it later—maybe in a few years.

Getting involved with Piper definitely feels like that. I've been ready all this time. The problem wasn't me. It was Skyla.

I don't even know if Piper wants children, but she damn sure knows I want them.

That's where this is going. That's why this is so important. She's the one. She's the only one—the only woman I've ever met whom I would ever even consider getting that serious about.

Her hand running down my back tells me so many things—so many secrets she never says in words.

It's a caring touch—almost like she wants to take care of me—like I'm the hurt one who needs extra special treatment.

She always does things like that. She always shows with little actions that she cares and she's thinking of me instead of herself.

She nuzzles her face into my side. Her breath warms me. "I hate that you have to go."

"You have to go, too," I murmur on the side. "You have to work today, remember?"

"I remember. Maybe I'll see you when you come for your meeting with Mitchell."

I don't want to think about my meeting with Mitchell. I want to stay with her. If I have to meet a lawyer at all, I want it to be her. At least I know I can trust her.

"I have to go." I bend over, roll her onto her back, and kiss her. I can't let her touch me or I'll never be able to pry myself away. "I'll call you tonight, okay? We can go out...or stay in..."

She laughs. She smiles more easily after last night. I just hope I gave her a little of what she gave me.

She wraps her arms around my neck to kiss me, but she doesn't have a problem letting me go. "Have a good day. Try not to scare the locals."

Now it's my turn to laugh. We don't talk about what's going to happen between me and Mitchell and the other lawyers. If they aren't scared of me yet, they will be after today.

I meet my limo driver at the curb outside. He drives me home where I take a shower, change my clothes, and get my game face on for the day ahead.

I stop by the office for a few hours of work before I go to Foster, Carraway, and Barnett. I don't see Piper on the way inside, but I don't look too closely.

I need to figure out how I'm going to proceed with her. I'd like to take her home and keep her there, but that obviously won't work when we both have to continue our careers.

I wouldn't want to interfere with her career anyway. She's too good and too highly regarded by everyone.

I go into Mitchell's office where I find the usual rowdy gang waiting for me. Of course Piper isn't here. They won't want her around sticking up for me. That would only make them look worse.

I sit down in my usual chair, but I already know what's coming.

"Your former wife's attorney sent over the settlement agreement this morning," Mitchell begins.

I raise my eyebrows like I'm really surprised. "Settlement agreement? Did you indicate to the other party that I was willing to settle—after I specifically told you I wasn't?"

He tries to wave that away. "It's only a matter of time before we settle on something. The only question is what terms we can negotiate in the process. The sooner we come to an agreement, the better the terms we can get."

"Answer my question, Mitchell," I snarl. "Did you or did you not indicate to the other party that I was willing to settle after I specifically ordered you not to?"

"Be reasonable," he insists. "The other party is willing to accept extremely favorable terms. She's only asking for a portion of stock in North Star Investments....."

I get to my feet. "You're fired, Mitchell. Your entire firm is fired. You're no longer representing me. No one from your firm will ever represent me again—and while I'm at it, I'll make sure none of my rich friends ever comes to you for representation again, either."

His eyes widen when he looks up at me. "But why? We're only doing our job. This is what representing you means—getting the best settlement for you."

"Consider your contract terminated. I expect you to destroy any copies of my confidential records and personal information you might still have in your possession. You are not empowered to negotiate this or any other matter on my behalf. If I find out you had any further communications with Skyla or her representatives, I'll sue you for fraud, slander, and defamation. Is that clear?"

Mitchell sits rooted to his chair with his eyes hanging out of their sockets. He really is too stupid to run a law firm if he doesn't understand why I'm giving him the boot.

The rest of his lackey partners stand around in frozen horror. Apparently I'm the first and only person to take issue with their methods.

I wait just long enough to make sure my words sink home. Then I walk out.

I shouldn't be surprised by this. I'm not surprised by this. I saw it coming at our last meeting. Now the only question is who I'm going to get to represent me in the divorce. I can only think of one person.

I go downstairs to Piper's office. Her eyes widen, too. "Take a walk with me," I tell her. "I need to talk to you."

"Is it business or personal?" she asks.

"Both."

I grab her hand and lead her outside. I don't want to talk to her inside the building. I don't want to talk to her even standing near the building.

I take her into a bakery next door. It's stifling hot and smells like burnt sugar.

"What's going on?" She looks up into my eyes with deep, drilling intensity. "Did something happen? What's wrong? Did something else happen with Skyla?"

"It wasn't Skyla. It was Mitchell. He and the other lawyers went behind my back and started negotiating to settle with her. They were going to give her stock in North Star Investments. I fired them. The firm no longer represents me—which means I need a different lawyer."

She blinks up at me. A million questions race through her mind.

"I need you, Piper," I murmur. "You're the only person I trust to represent me. You know everything about this case—and I'm still not even sure if Mitchell and the others read my documents. It has to be you. Can't you do this case on the side—independent from the firm? Or can't you go into private practice or something? You have an outstanding reputation. People come from all over the Tri-State area to work with you. You aren't accomplishing anything here except making Mitchell a bundle of money. You could go independent...."

She breaks away, turns her back on me, and paces across the bakery.

I don't go after her. I don't know if she ever considered going into private practice on her own. Don't ask me what I'll do if she turns me down.

She stands over there for a long time without looking at me. I want to shake her and force her to take me on, but I can't do that. I just have to let her come to this on her own—or not.

I don't even know if some ethical dilemma would stop her from representing someone she's involved with in a sexual relationship. That only makes sense, doesn't it?

She stays there for so long that I start to get worried. I have other appointments today. Should I leave and let her think about it?

She surprises me out of my mind by turning and marching straight up to me. She dips her chin once. "All right. I'll do it."

"You'll....do what? You'll represent me on the side or you'll quit the firm?"

"I'll quit the firm and go independent. You're right. This incident shows a glaring lack of integrity on the part of all the partners—but Mitchell especially. I knew they weren't as straight up as they appeared, but this really nails it. I could do better on my own—so I'll start with your case. We'll start first thing Monday morning."

I burst into a huge grin. I want to laugh. "Thank you! I'm so grateful!"

She beams at me. "You're welcome. You're right. You deserve better representation than they can give you. They had no right to negotiate when you ordered them not to."

"So......do we need to go back to pretending we don't have a relationship?"

Her cheeks color. "We do have a relationship—don't we? I don't know what relationship we have, but we do have one. Tell me I'm wrong."

"No, you aren't wrong. Is that going to be a problem? Don't you have rules against that?"

"It's fine as long as the lawyer and client are in an established relationship—like say if they're spouses or some other close personal relationship."

I freeze and stare at her. "Spouses?"

She turns bright red and laughs while she waves that away. "Never mind. We'll just go ahead with the case. I'll follow up with Skyla's attorney and inform them that the firm isn't representing you anymore. I'll tell them to forward all communication to me instead."

"Thank you, Piper," I choke. "You don't know what this means to me."

She squeezes my arm and beams up at me. "Yes, I do. That's why I'm doing it."

I have to put my arms around her. I don't care if we're in public.

She sinks into me. She never felt so good. Her arms slip around my waist and she buries her face in my chest.

I want to kiss her, but that can wait. Someday soon, our relationship will be established enough that I can kiss her in public without worrying about who's watching.

I satisfy myself by letting my lips fall on her hair. Her smell rushes into my nostrils and brings back a thousand memories from last night—her breasts in my mouth, her slippery juices on my fingers, her leg over my shoulder, her thighs around my face.....

That smell bursts my head apart and cracks my heart with aching emotion. I want her. I want her precious heart all to myself.

I never want to let go of her, but I have to. I'll see her tonight—and every other night. Then everyone will know she's mine and I'm hers. Then no one will question anymore and we'll both be free.

I start to relax my hold on her. I lean back and gaze down into her beautiful eyes.

She bursts into another matching smile gazing up at me.

Right at that moment, a pop, a flash, and a scream echo out of the kitchen behind the bakery wall.

I look up to see what the matter is, and in that instant, the whole kitchen detonates in a flaming ball of fire.

The wall explodes right in front of me. Instinct takes over and I grab Piper.

I crush her against my body to protect her. I barely have time to turn my back to the blast before it smashes into me from behind and knocks me flat on the floor.

Chapter 22: Piper

I cough dust and smoke out of my eyes, nose, and mouth. I try to squint to see where I am, but I can't see anything. It's pitch black.

"Judah....!" I choke. I can't see him, either. No one answers me. "Judah!!" I yell a little louder.

He coughs to my left. I try to scramble in his direction, but something heavy blocks me. It hangs directly over me just inches from my back.

A mountain of debris leaves a tiny hollow just barely big enough for me to fit under it. I have to lie flat on my stomach.

I try to claw my way to my left while I grope around on the floor. I call a little louder. "Judah....where are you?"

"Piper...." he rasps.

I scoot under the debris toward the sound of his voice. I paw through dust, rubble, and fallen plaster all over the floor.

I can't see a thing. I don't even know if I'm anywhere near Judah.

Just then, my hand touches his shoulder. "Judah!" I practically shriek. "Judah—can you hear me?! Talk to me!"

"I'm....I'm okay...." He sounds shaky—like he's just waking up.

I drag myself a little closer. It isn't easy with so much junk piled all over us.

I'm still clear in this little open place. I don't know about Judah. I hate to think of him getting crushed under all that falling debris.

I pull myself right up next to him and pat him down all over. I wish I could see him. I'll just have to do this by touch.

I pass my hand over his back. I don't find anything. I check lower. His legs are free, too. Nothing is holding him down.

I go back up to his head and touch his face and scalp. "Are you okay?" I pant. "Are you hurt anywhere? Talk to me. You're scaring m e."

"I'm okay, baby...." he croaks. "I think something hit me in the head....but I'm okay. Just give me a second."

I keep touching him all over the head. I find a patch of something warm and wet on the top corner of his temple.

"You're bleeding," I murmur. "We need to stop the bleeding. Can you turn over? Can you face me?"

"I'll.....I'll try.....My head is killing me."

"Just hold on," I gasp. "We're gonna get out of here."

I scramble for a way to stop the bleeding on his head. I don't even know how bad it is.

I can't think of anything to use but my shirt. I tear open my blazer, pull my shirt out of my waistband, and use my teeth to tear off the bottom edge. I fold it into a bandage and press it against his head.

He roars in pain when I put pressure on it. "I'm sorry!" I exclaim. "I just don't want you to lose too much blood. I don't know how long we'll be stuck in here."

"It's all right," he growls. "It just hurts."

"Are you sure you didn't get hurt worse than that?" I pat down his face again. I don't want to believe he really is all right.

He finally heaves himself up enough to roll onto his side facing me. I pat down his arms and body enough to feel that he's holding the fabric to his head.

"Thank you, baby," he mutters. "I'm sorry I scared you. I'm okay. I think I must have passed out for a second."

"I'm not surprised if you got hit in the head." I find my hands moving back to his face. Touching him is rapidly replacing looking at him. "I was worried you got crushed in the explosion."

He mumbles something and tries to lift his head before he puts it back down. "I wonder what caused it."

"It sounded like something caught fire or exploded in the kitchen before that one big explosion took out the whole bakery. I heard someone scream right before it happened and then a crash."

"I heard the same thing." He takes his arm down and then touches his head. "I don't think I broke any bones. It's just a gash."

"That's good. You didn't get hurt anywhere else, did you?"

"No, I'm fine." His tone changes. "Are you okay? Did you get hurt?"

"No, you protected me with your body, remember? Then I fell and all this debris fell in a way that made this little opening for us. It's holding up the rest of the bakery. That's the only way we survived."

His hands brush my face from out of the dark. "Piper......I love you."

I freeze at those words. Before I can do anything, his hands close around my face and he pulls me into his lips.

I sink into that kiss, and like magic, our bodies come together the same way they did last night.

He kisses me endlessly, deliciously—and in that kiss, I feel that he really does love me.

All this craziness with Skyla and the firm and Jasmine and everything—all those problems and obstacles just brought us closer together. We wouldn't be here without all of them.

Even Mitchell misrepresenting Judah brought us together. We wouldn't have been in the bakery right at that moment if Mitchell did his job.

I let myself ease closer to Judah in the dark. Dust, broken plaster, and gravel scrape on the floor underneath me, but I don't notice any of that.

I let my body sink into him the way it did last night. We might as well be in my bedroom.

"I want everything with you," he whispers. "I want to take you home with me and keep you there. I don't ever want you to leave."

I collapse into those lips—the lips that say those things about me—about us. My heart overflows with some powerful emotion. Is it love?

Kissing him like this isn't enough. I fall on top of him and feel the blessed relief of his arms around me. We're together even here.

His big, strong hand closes on my head to press me into his heart. I hear it pounding through his shirt. His body breathes for me under those clothes.

That body is mine to touch, mine to pleasure. I can slip my hands inside his clothes whenever I want and feel how magnetically strong, powerful, and attractive he is.

Just then, a shaft of light bursts into the darkness. Judah and I squint and look up toward the source.

"Is anyone in here?!" a man's voice calls. "Can anyone hear me?!"

"We're here!!" I yell and try to sit up. I hit my head on the fallen beams and broken ceiling over my head. "We're over here! My friend is hurt! He needs medical attention!"

"We're coming in!" the guy yells back. "We're from the Fire Department! We're going to get you out. We just need to stabilize the building. Just hold on!"

"They're coming for us!" I tell Judah. "We're getting out of here."

He laughs and then coughs. I can see him now.

The gash on his head doesn't look so bad. Dust covers his face, head, and suit. The dust turns him white, but he smiles up at me with the same warmth as always.

I can't help smiling back. "We're gonna be okay," I murmur.

He nods. "Yeah."

More light beams flicker into the darkness from the same direction. "Hold on!" the same guy yells. "We're bringing in a crane to lift this stuff off you. Just stay where you are."

I don't tell him we can't leave until they remove all the debris, but that doesn't matter. Judah and I lie side by side on the floor talking with our arms around each other. The Fire Department guys keep interrupting by yelling orders and instructions back and forth.

We stay where we are for an hour before one of the Fire Department guys yells inside, "You can come out now! Try to crawl toward us! The opening should be big enough for you to get out! Come on!"

"You go first," Judah tells me.

"No, you're the one who's hurt. You go first."

He laughs at me and rolls onto his stomach. He groans a lot while he pulls himself through the low hollow toward the Fire Department guys in the distance.

They keep shining their flashlights at us and yell encouragement that we're almost there and to keep going.

Judah makes it and they pull him out. Then they grab me.

I straighten up on the sidewalk outside. Some other firefighters are already taking Judah away to a waiting ambulance.

I don't get a chance to follow him or talk to him again. He glances over his shoulder in my direction before they put him inside and drive him away.

I stand stunned on the sidewalk while the firefighters and paramedics pat me down and bombard me with a million questions.

I stare across the street at the place where the ambulance used to be. Judah loves me….and I love him. I should have told him. I should have taken that moment to tell him.

He already knows, but I should have told him anyway.

What about the rest of it? Do I want to go home with him and stay there?

That house—the house where I lived with my husband—the house where my husband got shot—it's a tomb.

I realized last night that I need to do something else to break from my past. Sleeping with Judah or even loving Judah won't free me from this burden.

Moving out of that house will. Moving in with Judah will. Selling the house, all the furniture, and putting all the old pictures in storage will.

Then my dead husband won't be lurking around watching everything I do. I won't have to worry about whether he approves of me sleeping with another man.

Judah doesn't seem to mind, but I do. I don't want my dead husband looking over my shoulder for the rest of my life.

I shouldn't have let him look over my shoulder last night. That was so tasteless—taking Judah there and doing it with him in front of all those pictures. I only realize that now in hindsight. I don't want it to happen again.

The firefighters eventually finish checking me out. They tell me I can go home, but it's still only noon.

I take a cab to my house, throw my suit in the laundry, take a shower, and put on clean clothes so I can go back to the office. I don't plan to do any work.

I gather a few files, copy a few things onto a jump drive, and collect the rest of my possessions. I take one last look around my office. I'll never come back here. I didn't think I would ever quit the firm, but everything changes.

Everything in my life is changing, so why not this, too? It's time to sweep out the cobwebs and start over with a clean slate.

I go upstairs and knock on Mitchell's door. He calls from inside, "Come in!"

I go in and put my stack of files on his desk. "I'm resigning from the firm effective immediately," I tell him.

He blinks at me. "Um....what?"

"I'm out, Mitchell. I don't work here anymore. I quit. I'm gone. I'm done. You can assign other people to handle these cases."

"But....why?" he stammers. "You're one of our best lawyers. Isn't there anything we can do to convince you to stay?"

"I can't think of anything, no."

"But.....give me some explanation. What happened? I thought you were satisfied with your role here. I know we haven't promoted you to senior partner as fast as you probably would have liked. Maybe we can work something out,...."

"This has nothing to do with how fast you promoted me and I have been satisfied here. I've been happy here, but it's time to move on. I've decided to go out on my own and open my own practice."

"But....." he stutters. "You'll probably take our best clients with you. Most of our highest-paying clients only come in because you're here."

I make a strategic decision not to stick it in his face that I already know that. Judah can read the writing on the wall and so can I.

"I can't help that, Mitchell. Maybe if you and the other partners took better care of your clients, people might come to this firm for you instead of me."

"What is that supposed to mean?"

"Nothing." I turn away. "You have my resignation. I wish all of you the best. See you around sometime."

I walk out and head down to the parking garage. I get halfway there and realize....I feel pretty damn good. I just quit the firm. I'm going out on my own.

I get into my car, but I don't drive anywhere. I spend half an hour on my phone sending an email to all my current and former clients that I no longer work for Foster, Carraway, and Barnett.

I tell my clients that, if they want me to continue to represent them, or if they need representation in the future, I'll be working independently from now on and I'd be happy to help them with whatever they need.

My fingers tremble when I hit, *Send*. This is it. I'm breaking the last tie. Now I'm flying free without a parachute, a net, a plane, or any other means of support. It's sink or swim.

Chapter 23: Judah

I raise my glass and tap it against Kevin's. "Here's to Miles Reynolds, the craziest stamp collector this side of the Mississippi."

Kevin laughs. "It's a miracle he got anywhere in business at all. He was nuts over his stamps."

Everyone sits around The Billionaires' Club socializing, lounging on the couches, and talking about Miles. We just finished the memorial service. Now it's time to relax and remember the man who gave so much to all of us.

"Did you hear that Miles's sons sold his coin collection for over six million dollars?" Rory asks. "Maybe old Miles was onto something."

"He started collecting when he was only seven years old," Giovanni tells him. "That's over eighty years of collecting. All he had to do was put aside coins as they came out and they appreciated in value. We couldn't do that. It's too late for us."

"Did you know he had coins from the Roman Empire?" Diego Espinosa chimes in. "He even had some from ancient Egypt."

"He showed me the Roman one once," I tell them.

Everyone gasps and turns around to stare at me. "No way!" Kevin exclaims.

"He loved Judah," Dante interjects. "Judah was one of his favorites."

"I was not," I counter. "I just let him talk about his coins more than most people. That's the only reason he liked me."

"Did you hear his sons are putting his appraisal company up for sale?" Giovanni asks. "Who wants to be the lucky investor who buys it and takes it over?"

No one answers. Silence falls over the group and then Niko laughs. "You won't catch me buying it. Hell no. I'm a trucker, not an antique dealer."

The others laugh, too. No one offers any staggering price for Miles Reynolds's appraisal company.

I down the rest of my drink and stand up. "I gotta go. You boys get on home to your mamas before you get grounded."

Laughter follows me out of the room. "Take it easy, Judah!" Niko calls after me.

I meet my limo driver outside. He takes me to Piper's house, but all the windows are dark. She doesn't answer when I knock.

I pull out my phone and text her. *Where are you?*

She texts back. *I'm downtown talking to one of my other current clients. I resigned from the firm this afternoon after the explosion. I emailed all my clients to tell them the news. Five different people I was representing through the firm are quitting, too, so they can come with me. This is great, Judah! I'm going to make it!*

I laugh and text her back. *I'm happy for you. Can you meet me for dinner?*

She hesitates a split second. *Okay, but can you meet me downtown? I'll pick you up. Give me the address.*

She does. I can barely sit still on my way over there.

She meets me on the sidewalk holding a big stack of file folders and an even bigger grin. She bursts out in excited laughter when she gets into the limo.

"I never thought my clients would react this way!" she gasps. "I thought I'd have to start over from scratch."

"Why would you do that? You're the best." I kiss her on the cheek, but she's too over the moon about her new career.

"I just talked to Salvatore Gambetta about renting an office in his building—and I need to hire an assistant and maybe a receptionist, now that the firm isn't providing me with them anymore."

"I'm sure you'll work out all the details."

She spins around like she just remembered that I'm here. "Oh! I've been meaning to tell you. I followed up on Mitchell's proposed settlement."

I stiffen. "What proposed settlement?"

"Exactly. Apparently, he didn't get the proposed settlement from Skyla's attorney because she doesn't have one. She's either doing it all herself or some friend of hers is helping her—but she doesn't have representation—not legal representation, at least."

"Mitchell specifically said....."

"He said that to sway you. He wanted you to come to the table and start thinking about what you were willing to concede to wrap up the case. If you ask me, he's the one who wanted to reduce publicity. He didn't care so much about how the publicity impacted you—and I'm pretty sure he never read your documentation. I questioned him about it and he couldn't answer basic questions about your trust or the list of your assets."

"So what does that mean?"

"It means no one has mentioned settlement to Skyla. She doesn't think you're offering to settle the way Mitchell led you to believe she does. She doesn't even know about all this. As far as I can tell, she still thinks I'm representing you—or she doesn't know I got removed from representing you if that makes sense."

I stare at her and blink. "But.....that's great!"

She bursts out in another grin. "Yeah! We can just pick up the case where we left off. Mitchell didn't damage your position at all—not like that."

I grab her and kiss her. "Thank you! I'm so relieved that you're back on the case!"

She laughs, makes a stupid face, and changes her voice to make it as deep as possible. "I'm....back on the case!" Then she busts up laughing again. "This is going to be the best thing that ever happened to me. Thank you so much for suggesting it. I wouldn't have done it without you pushing me."

I find myself beaming at her reaction. She glows with excitement, happiness, and new life. It makes her a thousand times more attractive, but I still like her old seriousness just as much if not more.

It sure is nice to see her happy—almost as happy as I feel when I'm around her. The cloud lifts and I can see daylight again when I'm with her.

Just knowing she's here in my life makes me feel better.

Am I rebounding? Do I only feel this way about her because I'm going through a divorce?

Maybe, but I don't think so. I would feel this way about Piper even if I wasn't going through a divorce.

Why should I wait another two years to get together with her when she's right here in front of me?

She finally notices me again and her expression clears, too. "How did your day go—apart from getting blown up in a bakery?" She frowns, raises her eyes to my head, and touches my scalp. "Are you okay? They must not have kept you in the hospital."

"I'm fine. It's just a cut. It didn't even need stitches." I slip my arms around her. "They say it's a good thing that you stopped the bleeding when you did. Thank you."

I pull her in and kiss her. I can't get enough of her.

She responds by melting in my arms, slipping her hands behind my neck, and her breath lengthens as the energy takes her. Desire pulses through her body instantly and she pushes her breasts against my suit.

I start to pull her into my lap, but just then, the limo draws up in front of the restaurant. It's The Aquarian on Park Avenue.

I don't want to stop kissing her. Her slim hands caress my face and brush my ears. She actually makes me feel beautiful when she touches me like this. I can start to believe that I might be as fine as she says I am

.

My hands take over. They start to crawl up her body toward her blazer. I have to tear myself away. "Later," I tell her.

She laughs again. She must be really happy if she's laughing this much.

We get out and go inside to our table. I want to hold her hand across the table, but looking at her is just as good.

"I contacted Jasmine Delvini about an hour ago," she tells me. "I sent her the paperwork for her deposition, so we should have that on file pretty soon. We can put that accusation to rest right away."

"We don't have to spend our dinner date talking about my case."

She blushes, but she won't stop grinning. "Sorry. I'm just busting at the seams. I thought you would want to know that we can forget about that part of Skyla's countercomplaint, at least."

"What do you want to do about the one against you?" I ask.

She shrugs it away. "Nothing I guess. She can't substantiate it, so it doesn't mean anything."

"So....it really doesn't bother you?"

"Not anymore." She pauses and studies me across the table. "It used to, but now I see it as a good thing. I mean, we wouldn't be where we are now without that accusation, would we? We have her to thank for all of this."

I can only gaze across the table at her face radiating so much light and enthusiasm and clarity.

She's right. I do have Skyla to thank for all of this. So many good things are coming into my life right now. I have Skyla to thank for all of them.

"I just don't want her accusation to harm you—in any way," I tell her. "Your reputation is going to be even more important, now that you're going out on your own."

She makes a face. "I wouldn't worry about that. Mitchell was the one who took me off your case because of that accusation. I don't see that the accusation would have made any difference to the case at all if he'd just left me in place. He could have made the opposite call and supported me. What difference would it have made in the end? If anything, his actions made it look even more like there might be something to her claim." She shrugs again. "It doesn't matter because it's over and I'm representing you again—so it all worked out in the end"

I have to admire her resilience. She just lets it roll off. She doesn't let it affect her or beat her down. This woman is truly exceptional.

Chapter 24: Piper

Judah opens the limo door for me. I slip inside and he climbs in after me.

The driver shuts the door and Judah and I move together automatically. I dissolve in his kiss as a river of bliss takes hold of me. It washes me away in such a warm sea of happiness and passion that I feel myself losing my grip on reality.

I can do that because I'm in his arms. He pulls me onto his lap and sits me sideways while we kiss.

I can touch his magnificent face, his head, stroke his neck, and I feel the muscle straining under his shirt when I slip my hand under his jacket.

His arms flex when he slides his hand between my thighs. I gasp in an agony of desire as his fingers crawl higher up my legs toward my panties.

His powerful arm supports me behind my back. I lie back trembling with anticipation for the rush of pleasure I know he's going to give me.

His hard spike digs into me from below. He tightens his grip on me to rub me against that throbbing bulge. I already feel the rhythm of his thrusts plunging into me and carrying me to the stratosphere.

He breaks away from my mouth and dives in to bite my neck. I let out a little scream as explosive electricity races up to my ear and spreads to the rest of my body.

My eyes float open trying to keep up with all the mind-blowing sensations he's giving me....and then I notice where we are.

The driver isn't heading uptown toward my house. He's pulling onto the Queensboro bridge.

"Um.....Judah....." I stammer.

He mumbles something into the side of my neck.

"Where are we going?" I try to bend over to see out the window. He doesn't make it easy when he's holding onto me so tightly. I wind up turning around on his lap so I can see out the window.

"We're going to my place," he tells me. His hands circle my waist and he pulls my ass down onto his lap. I'm facing away from him now.

"Your place?!" I exclaim.

"We spent the night at your place last night. Now we're going to my place." He hauls me another few inches backward—right down on his rigid shaft plowing into me from below.

He scoops his hands up to my breasts, squeezes from behind, and then down between my legs, but my skirt gets in the way.

Another blast of excruciating desire hits me, but just as fast, he sits back on the seat and lets go. "I thought you would want to, but I can take you home if you want me to."

I try to turn around, but that only teases me on his spike even more.

"I do want to," I tell him. "I just....I didn't expect it."

He cools right away. He kisses me, lifts me off his lap, and sits me on the seat next to him. "Don't worry about it. It's just a house. I don't have rooms full of stuffed animals staring at you."

I laugh, but that only reminds me of my house. I really need to change that before I ask Judah to go back there.

All those pictures of me and my late husband seem so creepy now. What in the world was I thinking?

I wasn't thinking I would get involved with anyone. I was thinking I *wouldn't* get involved with anyone. That's why I kept the house the way it was.

Judah faces front on the seat. Our make-out session is over—for now.

I can't stop bubbling with desire for him, though. I want to touch him. He's still hard. I can see that, but he won't start anything—not here—not in the car.

He'll wait until we get to his house. Then he'll start up again. He can wait.

I don't want to wait. I want to do it here—in the car. I want so many things with him.

I lean in and kiss him. He kisses me back, but he doesn't paw at my body or put me on his lap again. That moment has passed.

I can accept that, but I can't accept just stopping—not when he turns me on this much.

I'm in his car with his handprints all over me. He just had his fingers creeping up my thighs. I don't want to stop.

I kiss him a little deeper and slip my hand between his legs. He stiffens when I touch him. His chest and stomach contract. He keeps kissing me, but his whole body tenses at my touch.

I love that. I love giving him that and showing him how hot he is.

I follow the length of his shaft as it swells inside his shorts. Mmmm. He feels so damn good. I want more.

I glide my lips off his mouth and bury my face in his lap. I nibble him through his pants and bite just a little harder while I unbuckle his belt.

His hand lands on the back of my neck. He doesn't make a sound or even hardly breathe until I get him in my mouth.

Then he gasps in ragged ecstasy and a deep shudder of pleasure and satisfaction trembles through him when I start to suck.

His massive heat floods my brain. The feeling of my lips gliding over him disintegrates my being. He feels amazing in my mouth.

His hand tightens a little bit more on the back of my neck—not enough to hurt or to control my movements.

He groans again and then sucks his breath between his teeth when I slither my tongue around his shaft. His power radiates through me from every part of his body.

"Oh, yeah," he whispers. "Oh, hell yeah, baby."

I love the sound of that tortured whisper urging me to pleasure him.

He strokes his hand down my back to my ass, squeezes, follows my hips when I push my ass into his hand, and then runs his hand back up my spine to my neck.

The radiant power of his hunger consumes me the way it did in the bar. He thrills me to the core just by being here—just by being so powerfully, mind-blowingly male.

His veins and flesh strain in my mouth. Every inch of him stretches taut as I suck faster, but he doesn't try to hurry up and end it.

He sits back savoring the pleasure I'm giving him. He keeps murmuring encouragement to me and following my movements with his hand on the back of my neck.

That hand feels masterful and always supremely in control. I can release all my stress and concern in that hand. I don't have to think or be anything except right here between his legs.

He raises his hand and strokes my hair for a minute. "We're almost there, baby," he murmurs.

I look up at him and run my tongue one last time around his throbbing length.

He smiles down at me so beautifully. He caresses my cheeks and uses the flat pad of his thumb to wipe the saliva off my lips. His eyes gleam with so much pleasure and happiness.

"You can do that when we get there," he tells me and smiles even more broadly. "You can do that anytime."

He lifts me back onto the seat and starts buttoning his pants while the limo swivels into a long, wooded driveway leading up to his house.

I'm not astounded by the size and grandeur of his house because I've seen pictures and floor plans of it in his divorce documentation. It sure looks nice in real life, though.

We pass the gate with security guards standing out front. They exchange a few words with the limo driver and then the car swings around in front of the entrance.

Judah gets out of the limo first.....and then I get out.

I stop dead in the driveway looking around at the grounds, the house, the ten-car garage to one side, and the equestrian barn tucked in the trees behind the house.

I turn in a complete circle taking it all in. The pictures don't do it justice.

Judah comes to my side and takes my hand. "Come inside," he murmurs in my ear. "You can look at everything from in there."

He leads me up the steps and into the giant entrance foyer. Hanging plants and potted trees rise to the skylight windows high above. Sweeping staircases run up both sides to the upper levels and the wings going off to both sides.

Seeing it on paper doesn't come close to seeing it in real life. I stop there to stare before I dare to venture deeper inside.

The entrance foyer opens into a glass conservatory overgrown with tropical plants. That opens onto the back terraces leading out to the grounds.

I can't look at all of that. I can't wrap my head around it all right now—not when I think about what this means.

Judah wants me to stay here. Can I really do that?

Some part of me still clings to my old life—the safe, easy, mummified life of my past.

I've already broken that link. Going back would mean death to me now.

I stop in front of the giant windows looking out over the grounds behind the house.

The trees form a border between the estate and all the other houses nearby. I can't see them. The trees erase the other houses and the city from my awareness. Judah and I are all alone here.

He comes up behind me and wraps his arms around my waist from behind. He sinks his mouth into my neck and all that simmering passion overflows in a river of lava between my legs.

My body stretches into him in aching, ravenous hunger. I need him. I need everything he's going to do to me, including breaking me away from the past. I need all of that.

His hands take hold of me in all their power. He rakes at my clothes, tugs up my skirt, tears my blazer open to maul my breasts through my blouse, and then yanks my buttons open so he can rip down my bra.

I want that. I want him to attack me. I want him to unleash his primal frenzy on me and burn down this wreck of a life I've been living all these years.

I gasp and moan in torrential desire. He can't touch me fast enough or hard enough. I try to shove his hand down between my legs, but he's already clawing at me too fast anyway.

He strips my shirt open to expose my nipples to the air. He bites me on the back of the neck and growls in such a brutal, animalistic voice that I scream. He's taking me. He's going to own me if he doesn't own me already.

He shoves me against the window. I have to flatten my arms against it just to give myself enough room to breathe.

Every breath comes out as a moan. He drills his spike into me from behind. I'm the one who made him that hard.

I sucked him. I turned him on and now I can't put the animal back in its cage. I don't want to put it back in its cage. I want it to ravage me and brutalize me and take me.

Judah's powerful hand claws up my back to my hair. He grabs a fistful of it in one cruel hold and then scratches down my back.

He grabs my blazer and blouse collar and strips both halfway down my back. He exposes my torso down to my ribs. My sensitive nipples touch the cold, unforgiving glass.

That feeling skyrockets me into a dizzy frenzy. I can't get enough when he pulls up my skirt, seizes one of my thighs to raise it aside, and plows into me from behind.

His hot breath husks in my ear in low, ragged growls. His body arches against me smashing me against the window.

I try to push off with my hands, but he doesn't let me. The world of nature and beauty out there bears witness to my ravishment and utter surrender to his power.

Chapter 25: Judah

I flex my hips to drive into Piper's sweet, juicy channel. Her inner muscles clamp around me every time I drill in deep.

Then those spongy soft layers quiver when I pull out for another thrust.

She feels so addictively good around me, but that's nothing compared to the way she looks laying on her back beneath me.

Her milky white arms stretch above her head to raise her breasts toward me. I can kiss them, suck them, bite them, or just lean back and watch them sway and bounce every time I pound into her.

Her thighs and ass spank with the rhythm of my thrusts. If I turn her over, she'll arch her ass to meet me. She matches everything I do with perfect surrender.

I can take her all night in every room in every position I can think of—and I have. I've been taking her all night and she still keeps going with no sign of exhaustion.

If she starts to fade, I only have to kiss her or eat her or finger her to make her escalate again. If I start to fade, she crawls between my legs and she won't leave me alone until she gets me hard again.

I never want to stop. I want to feel this incredible sense of mastery and domination surging through me all the time.

I want to see her twisting her face away and grimacing in tormented ecstasy. I want to listen to her howl as each cataclysm sweeps her out of this world.

I love hearing her scream like that for me, hearing her beg for me, and watching her shudder when I take her.

I don't see how this can ever end. I don't see how I can even stand to pull out of her long enough to go to work even though I know I have to.

Just then, my phone starts ringing on the floor. The phone is in my pants pocket on the bedroom carpet where I tossed them last night—while I was conquering her.

I dive in and give her a kiss before I sit back, lean over the bed, and pick up my pants. I check the phone, but I already missed the call.

She crawls up behind me and starts kissing me all over my back. Her wicked little fingers drag up and down my thighs. "Do you have to go to work today?" she mumbles between kisses.

"Of course I do, baby, and so do you. Don't think you're going to stay in bed all day now that you're independent."

She laughs and flops back on the bed all naked and glowing and beautiful. She smirks at me while she writhes her glorious body in front of my eyes. "Are you sure about that?"

"You're a bad girl and you know what happens to bad girls." I grab her, flip her on her stomach, and deliver a quick smack to each of her ass cheeks.

She shrieks and then explodes with laughter again. "Aaargghh! Beat me harder, you savage!"

Now it's my turn to laugh. "Don't tempt me. I'm going to take a shower. Try not to melt into a puddle on the sheets before I get back."

"I think I already did." She laughs again.

That sound follows me out of the room. I never imagined getting together with her would turn out to be this fun. We're both usually so serious.

We can only act this way because we're alone together—and because we're serious all the rest of the time. This doesn't change who we are—or maybe it does. Maybe this is the start of a completely new me.

I take a shower, but when I get back to the bedroom, she isn't there.

I find her in the kitchen making breakfast in one my T-shirts and nothing else. It barely comes down to the crease of her ass. It makes her look absolutely blistering hot.

I shove up behind her and start to bend her over the kitchen counter. That ass calls to me and grabs me by the nuts.

I start to get hard for her, but she breaks away, pushes a tall glass of iced cappuccino into my hands, and runs off laughing to the bathroom.

I have to adjust my junk in my shorts so I can sit down at the kitchen counter and eat the breakfast she left out for me.

I love that I'm the one who gets to see her like this. I bet no one from Foster, Carraway, or Barnett ever imagined her wearing nothing but a man's oversized T-shirt and running around bare-assed with her hair all messy and laughing in that sexy, teasing way.

She does it for me. She teases me like that with her beautiful, ripe butt cheeks peeking out from under the shirt hem.

I'm going to have a hard time concentrating on work today, but I can get through it. I can bite the bullet because I know I'll have her again. I'll bring her back here and she'll be mine in my bed for whatever I want to do with her.

She comes out with her hair combed, her makeup done, her heels on, and wearing her business suit. Playtime might be over, but she gives me a wild smirk when she catches me checking her out. Christ, I need this woman!

She kisses me long and deep before she eats breakfast. "I need to go back to my house," she tells me. "I'll have to set up a temporary home office there until the rental on my new one starts—and I have files and stuff there that I need to use."

"I'll send you in a different car," I tell her. "I need to go straight to work."

She smiles at me. "Okay. Whatever works for you."

"Come over again tonight," I tell her. "We'll have dinner here this time."

She bursts into another blushing grin. "I'd love to, but let's try to get some sleep tonight."

"Sleep—what's that?"

She laughs again, kisses me, and we separate at the door.

I call another limo service to come and pick her up to take her home. I get into my limo and drive off. I feel no reservations at all about leaving her alone in my house. I wish I could get her to move in.

I start fantasizing about how I can make it happen. To hell with getting her to move in. I want to marry her. I want her to be the mother of my children.

That sounds so cheap when I'm still in the middle of divorcing Skyla. Now I understand why Piper wanted to take it slower. I guess I can wait on that—but only as long as I have Piper in the meantime.

I should wait at least until the divorce is final before I ask Piper to move in for good. After that, I suppose I'll have to wait a certain amount of time before I'm free to marry again.

That's okay. I can wait as long as it takes for this—and I don't want her to feel rushed. I want her to feel as safe and happy as she does right now. I don't want to threaten her independence.

I gaze out the window and start dreaming about last night. I have to be careful that I don't go into the office as hard as a rock.

I'm going to have to work to get that image of her in my T-shirt out of my mind. I never want to forget that. That T-shirt is going to be my new favorite outfit to see her in.

I smirk to myself thinking that, but right at that moment, the limo drives over a pothole and jolts me back to reality.

I glance through the front windshield. The driver is just pulling onto the highway. He picks up speed to put the miles behind us on our way to Manhattan.

I go back to thinking about Piper. This is why I ride everywhere in a limo—so I can think while someone else drives.

A slam startles me out of another smoky fantasy. I look up front and see the driver wrestling the wheel.

At the same moment, the limo veers and almost goes off the road. "What's wrong?!" I call through the window.

"The brakes just failed!" he yells back. "I can't slow down!"

I lunge forward in my seat. "That's impossible! You just took the car in for service last week!"

"I know!" he hollers back. "Just hold onto something! I'm gonna try to slow it down by riding against the barricade. This could get bumpy!"

I sit back in the seat wishing I could strap myself into some kind of safety harness, but I can't do that.

He fights the wheel for another minute and then steers off the highway onto the shoulder.

A heavy-duty concrete barrier separates the highway from a steep drop to the ground below. The driver slams the limo's side against the barricade.

Deafening shrieks of tearing metal rip through the car as it grinds down the length of the barricade. His maneuver works to slow the car down, but we're going too fast and it takes too long.

The barricade comes to a sudden stop and the car careens off the highway, tips violently, and plunges nose first into the pavement thirty feet below.

Chapter 26: Piper

I have to stop and stare at the long, sleek, black limo pulling up in front of Judah's house. He isn't here. He already left for work.

He ordered this car for me. I would be riding in these limos all the time if we....

I shake that thought out of my head. I don't know where Judah and I are going, but it sure looks like we're going somewhere.

He said he wants that and I know he's serious. I just don't know about myself.

I dread going back to my house. That house is in my past now. I know that, but it will still take me some time to rebuild something else. I don't know if that will be with Judah, but it will be somewhere else.

His life is so luxurious. Am I ready for that? Am I ready to be considered his next trophy?

Other people might see it that way, but he never would. I'm certain of that. He doesn't see me that way. He isn't interested in me for my looks even though he is—kind of.

I don't know what I think about Judah, but I know what I have to do about my career. I still have seven client cases to deal with, including his.

The limo takes me back to Manhattan and drops me off in front of my house. This place feels ancient and funereal compared to Judah's massive, sprawling estate.

I take a deep breath and go inside. I have to resist the urge to dump all my husband's pictures in a box before I start work.

I don't feel him judging me for spending the night with Judah. I don't feel my dead husband judging me even for spending the night with Judah in this house.

I just don't want to look at those pictures anymore. I don't want to think about them. They represent a past that doesn't belong to me anymore.

I distract myself by getting to work. I go through all my files, do a bunch of research, make a bunch of phone calls, and set a bunch of appointments to meet my clients at my new office.

I can't start using it for another week. Then I'll need to get furniture, staff—the works.

I get another thrill when I think about buying my own office furniture and hiring my own staff. This is going to be great. Thank you, Judah—again.

I have to go to the law library to look up a few things, so I leave at an hour later. I'm walking down the steps getting my car keys out of my purse when I spot Skyla coming toward me from down the block.

I skid to a halt and brace myself for the confrontation I know is coming.

She glares at me and clamps her mouth shut crossing the last dozen yards.

"Hi, Skyla," I breeze. "What brings you to this side of town?"

"I know you spent the night with Judah," she snaps. "I know you brought him here and spent all night with him, you tramp. Don't lie about it."

I sigh. "I don't have to lie about it, Skyla. I'm not ashamed of it. I'm proud of it."

"You keep away from my husband!" she rages. "You keep your filthy hands off him!"

Her reaction makes me deadly calm. I don't have to fly off the handle. She's doing just fine for both of us.

"He isn't your husband anymore, Skyla. You threw him away. You had him and you squandered him by cheating on him with hundreds of other men. You would have been set for life, but you just couldn't stop working the streets and turning tricks."

"You stole him from me!" she bellows. "You ruined our marriage! We would be happy if you just stayed away from him!"

She obviously has some mental health issues, but I'm all done with her. I don't need this shit.

"Do you know who ruined your marriage, Skyla? You did. Do you really want to know who made it possible for me and Judah to get together? You did. We wouldn't be together at all if not for you—so thank you."

"You lying bitch! I never did anything to put you and Judah together."

"You accused him of cheating with me. The partners of my law firm took me off his case so I wasn't his lawyer anymore. I wouldn't have been able to get together with him if you only kept your mouth shut."

She gasps in horror. "How dare you?!"

"I feel sorry for you. He's an exceptional man. He's a real prize. You had him. He loved you. He was totally loyal to you, but you just couldn't keep him. You had it all and now you have nothing. Now you just have to stand aside and watch while someone else shows him what he's really worth. Don't worry. I'll treat him right. You'll never have to worry about me hurting him the way you did because I would never do that. So thank you. Thank you for giving me Judah. I really appreciate your thoughtfulness."

I turn on my heel and walk away from her. She stays standing on the street corner and watches me out of sight.

I'm walking away from where I should be going to get my car, but I don't want her to see me walking toward her. I want to twist the knife by turning my back on her.

She's got some nerve calling Judah her husband or accusing me of stealing him from her—as if she didn't do enough on her own to drive him away.

It's a miracle he can get with anyone after the way she treated him, but that doesn't matter because I don't have to worry about her. She'll never be able to come between me and Judah the way she claims I came between them.

I make it halfway down the block. I'm just making up my mind to walk all the way around the block and come up behind her to get my car.

Just then, my phone rings in my purse. I glance behind me before I answer it, but Skyla isn't there anymore.

The screen reads, *Unknown Number.* That's strange.

I answer it. "Hello?"

"Piper Lagrange?" a deep male voice asks.

"Yes, I'm Piper Lagrange. Who is this?"

"Detective Andreas Beckett of the NYPD."

I stiffen. "Um....okay. What is this all about?"

"I believe you know Judah Hayes. He's in the hospital after a serious car accident."

I gasp out loud. "Oh, my God! Is he okay?"

"He will be. He's been unconscious following a head injury, but the medical team says it's nothing serious. He just woke up asking for you.

Do you need a ride to the hospital? I can send out a squad car to pick you up."

"Um...." I scramble to look all around me. "I have a car. I'm on my way now. Which hospital is he in?"

Detective Beckett gives me the address. I drop everything, jump in my car, and burn rubber to the hospital as quick as I can.

I find Judah lying on a hospital bed with his eyes closed. He looks fragile and vulnerable like this.

Two men stand by his bed. One is a uniformed police officer with a radio clipped to his shoulder. The other wears a secondhand suit, loafers, and no tie, but he looks strong and healthy under his jacket.

He turns his sharp green eyes at me when I walk in. "Ms. Lagrange? I'm Detective Beckett."

I barely look at him. I can't tear my eyes away from Judah. "What happened? How did the accident happen?"

"That's what I was hoping to ask you."

I spin around to stare at the detective. "Me! You want to ask me about it? Why?"

"Someone tampered with the brake lines of Mr. Hayes's car. The driver barely managed to slow the car down before it ran off the road. I understand you were at Mr. Hayes's house last night."

"I was at his house with him!" I have to fight my voice under control. "I was with him all night. I didn't tamper with his car!"

"I'm not saying you did, Ma'am," Detective Beckett murmurs with saintlike patience. "Mr. Hayes already told us you were with him all night. I'm asking if you saw anything while you were there—anything out of the ordinary."

I struggle to think straight. I didn't see anything because I was so out of my mind with pleasure and orgasmic bliss. I barely saw Judah last night. My vision wasn't working right.

I don't tell the detective that, though. I just mumble, "I didn't see anything."

"What about this morning before you left? I understand Mr. Hayes left first. Then you left in a different car."

"He left in his own limo. He ordered a different one to take me home. His own driver was driving the limo. Why don't you ask him? He would have been around the car more than I would have. He would have seen anything unusual if there was anything unusual to see."

Detective Beckett shifts his weight to his other foot. "Unfortunately, the driver got killed in the crash. The car tipped off a ledge and smashed nose first into the pavement twenty feet below the highway. I can't ask the driver anything. That's why I'm asking you."

I take another shaky breath and pass my hand across my forehead. "I'm sorry. I shouldn't have reacted like that."

"That's quite all right, Ma'am. So....did you see anything?"

"No, everything about the car and the driver looked normal when Judah left. The car didn't show any sign of any problems when it pulled out of the driveway. That was the last time I saw them."

"Okay. Thank you, Ma'am. We'll be looking into this. We'll let you know if we have any other questions."

Chapter 27: Piper

I approach Judah's hospital bed slowly and stare down at his sleeping face.

He's so big, but he looks soft and broken like this. Seeing him hurt makes me want to take care of him.

I don't have to think too hard to figure out who did this to him. I can only think of one person who would want to hurt Judah like this.

My experience with my husband comes back to haunt me. Skyla must be out of her mind if she thinks I'm threatening her relationship with Judah. There is no relationship to threaten. She ended it.

She's obviously too delusional to see that. She still thinks they have a chance to be happy together. She thinks I'm the one coming between them.

This is a replay of my husband's killer, but this time is different because it's Judah. He really was married to Skyla.

She had him and she threw him away. What a fool. She doesn't even realize what she had.

I realize because now I have it—at least I think I do.

I really want it. I don't want what he had with her, but I want something real.

We have something real. I know that now. I just have to overcome all these mental blocks and take it.

I can't let what happened with Skyla happen with me. I can't throw him away. He's too good for that. He's too pure and exceptional.

I sit down on the edge of his bed and stroke his cheek. He's so fine and strong. My heart overflows with emotion for him.

I want to show him what a relationship can really be like. I want to show him what it's like to love someone who cares for him, takes care of him, and gives him everything.

I want to erase Skyla from his mind. I want to fill him with happiness—the happiness I've seen in him these last few days.

If I can give him that, I don't want anything to stop me from spreading that to his whole life. He deserves that. He doesn't deserve some tramp from the other side of town doing him wrong and turning his life into a disaster zone.

He stirs when I touch him. He groans and turns his head the other way. He takes a deep breath, scowls, opens his eyes, and then collapses on the pillow with his eyes shut again when he sees me.

"Piper..." he husks. "You're here."

"I'm here. I came as soon as I heard. How are you feeling?"

"My head is killing me. The limo....crashed."

"I know." I lean in and kiss him. "Everything's okay now."

His eyes snap open and he looks around. "Carl......Is Carl okay?"

"Who's Carl?"

"My driver. He was trying to control the car....."

"I'm sorry, sweetheart. He didn't make it."

He throws himself down with a roar of agony like a wounded animal. He thrashes on the bed snarling through his teeth. "Aarggh! You rotten bitch!"

I press his hand. I already know who he's talking to and it isn't me.

I stroke his knuckles and rub his chest. It takes him a few minutes to settle down, but he won't stop clenching his teeth and glaring at different parts of the room.

"Detective Beckett told me about someone tampering with your car," I tell him.

Judah doesn't answer. He lies there fuming in rage.

I don't mind. He has every right to be angry.

I take his hand again. "Let's get out of here. I'll take you home."

He looks away. "How long do I have to stay in here?"

"I'll find out for you." I stand up and kiss him on the forehead above his eyebrow. I don't know what part of his head hurts. He could be surly for a while.

I check with the nurses and find out they plan to release Judah in a few hours. I field a few phone calls in the waiting room and cancel all the appointments I made for today.

My clients are much more understanding now than they would have been when I worked for Foster, Carraway, and Barnett. I can redo my schedule whenever I want. They expect it because I'm independent.

I go back to Judah's room to find him sitting a little farther upright. Someone has propped up his bed so he's almost vertical.

"I'm sorry I went off just now," he growls when I sit down next to him.

"It's okay. I feel the same way. The question is how we're going to pin it on her."

He grumbles under his breath, "I guess the cops are already investigating it."

"Something might turn up."

He snorts, but not even that can dampen how happy I am to be here with him. I just want to be with him, even if he's angry, even if he's hurting. I want to be with him especially if he's angry or hurting.

I don't seem to be able to stop myself from stroking his forehead, scalp, cheeks, and neck. "Tell me if you want me to stop. I don't want to make your headache worse."

"It feels good," he mutters. "Your hands are cold. It makes my head hurt less."

I beam at him and press my hand harder against his forehead. "Like this?"

He takes hold of my wrist and moves my hand slighter farther toward his temple. "Here."

I gaze down at him from inches away. He never looked more mesmerizing than he looks right now. Every pore of his skin looks carved out of some heavenly dark cloud.

I kiss him on the forehead, and just as fast, he cups both my cheeks in his hands and pulls my mouth down to kiss me. "Thank you for coming," he murmurs.

"Of course I came. I wouldn't be anywhere else."

He runs his fingers through my hair, but just then, the nurse comes in with his release paperwork.

He grumbles and complains a lot when he sits up and puts his feet on the floor to sign the paperwork. Then he has to get dressed

I wait for him to finally stand up. He hobbles out to the car.

I open the passenger door for him to get in. The minute he collapses into the seat, he pulls the lever and folds the seat all the way back so he can lie down flat. He shuts his eyes and doesn't open them all the way back to his house on Long Island.

The security guard at the gate holds up his hand to stop me in the driveway. I roll down the driver's window. "Can I help you, Ma'am?" he asks. "This is a private residence."

Before I can answer, Judah sits up in the passenger seat and calls over to the guard. "It's me, Charlie. She's driving me home."

"Yes, Sir, Mr. Hayes," the guard replies. "I apologize, Ma'am. I didn't see him."

He opens the gate and I drive in. I park in front of the house and Judah drags his sad, pathetic ass upstairs to the bedroom where he sprawls immediately.

"I'm sorry I'm not very good company right now," he grumbles.

"Don't worry about it. I did say we should get some sleep tonight."

He cracks his eyes open just enough to make contact with mine. "I want you."

I chuckle under my breath and bend over him to kiss him on the cheeks and eyebrows. "Just get better. I'm not going anywhere."

I try to keep my kisses gentle, but out of nowhere, he raises one hand and squeezes my breast through my suit. "Judah!" I squeal.

He pulls me down into his mouth and weasels his hand up my skirt. "Just a little taste, baby. Just for a minute."

I yelp when he starts rubbing me, but when he sits up enough to try to nuzzle my chest, he winces and falls back on the pillow rubbing his forehead. "Aaah! Or maybe not."

I laugh at him, but I try not to laugh too hard. "Just get your strength back. You'll be back on the horse soon enough."

"I'll be back on the horse riding you."

I giggle and blush at him, but he obviously can't start anything in his condition.

I push him down on the bed, kiss him on the forehead again, and go down to the kitchen to make lunch for both of us.

When I take the food up to his room, I find him asleep again. I stand by his bed gazing down at him. I've never seen him like this before.

He looks peaceful—like a peacefully sleeping angel—a big, black angel with bulging muscles, tree-trunk thighs, and six-pack abs.

His face never looked more perfectly carved out of dark brown granite. I admire every slope of his eyebrows, cheekbones, and the dome of his head.

I sit down on the couch across the room, eat my lunch, and work on my phone for a while. I don't want to disturb Judah.

This feels so nice—just being here with him while he recovers. I don't need anything else.

Chapter 28: Judah

I wake up to see late afternoon sunshine streaming through my bedroom windows. I've been asleep most of the day.

I sit up and spot Piper sitting on the couch across the bedroom. She must have been here all day, too.

A tray of food sits on the nightstand next to me. She must have made it for me.

She looks up from her phone and a bunch of file folders. She smiles at me. "Hey! How are you feeling?"

I nod. "I feel better. I feel like taking you out to dinner."

Her eyes pop out. "Are you sure you're up for that?"

"Of course I'm up for it. I'm not dead or in the hospital."

"You might as well be."

I don't take the joke. "Come on. Let's go out to dinner."

I stand up and flinch when another knife of white pain stabs me in the head. I rub my eyebrow and head for the closet.

"Are you sure you can handle this right now? We don't have to. You said you wanted to have dinner here."

"No, I want to go out—unless you don't want to."

"I don't mind one way or the other as long as I'm with you."

I'd like to kiss her and get a lot more things started with her, but one thought keeps nagging at my mind. Skyla killed Carl. She could have killed me. She tried to kill me.

I can't stay home with this hanging over my head. I need to get out. I need to move around. I need to do something before this information makes me explode.

I call the limo service to send me another car and driver—just for tonight. I'll have to rotate them so Skyla doesn't get any more stupid ideas.

She clearly already is getting plenty of them if she can go this far.

We stop by Piper's house so she can grab a few things. Neither of us mentions the obvious subtext.

If she's staying at my place long enough to need a bag of her clothes, toothbrush, hair gear, and laptop, she might as well stay indefinitely—but we aren't having that conversation—not yet.

We go out to a restaurant—The Albion, this time.

I feel myself stewing with rage. I really need to shut it down so I can concentrate on her tonight, but she doesn't seem to mind.

She holds my hand in the back of the limo and doesn't try to talk to me. I can't even appreciate how spectacular she looks in a slim beige dress that hugs every sweeping curve.

My resentment toward Skyla even dampens my desire to touch Piper. I don't want to do something I'll regret later. I'm really not in any mental space to be taking her out.

We get a table near the windows overlooking the river. Lights gleam on the water out there. This should be a romantic setting, but I can't enjoy it.

I'm too busy hating Skyla to notice anything until Piper picks up my hand off the table. She cradles it in both of hers and pets her smooth palm across my knuckles.

"Can I ask you something?" she asks.

"Absolutely," I tell her. "Ask me anything."

"Do you remember when you said you wanted to take me home and keep me there?"

"Yes. I remember."

"Do you still feel that way?"

"Of course I do." I shut my eyes and shake my head, but that only gives me another blinding stab of pain behind my eyes. "I'm sorry I'm brooding so much tonight. This was a bad idea."

"I was wondering....if you still feel that way.....if I could move in with you."

My head shoots up. The question surprises me so much I barely notice another sickening blast of pain.

I blink at her. I can barely make myself heard. "Do you really mean it?"

She nods, but her features pinch with her own inner pain. "I don't mean to spring this on you if you aren't ready...."

"Of course I'm ready! I thought you weren't ready. I thought you wanted to take it slow. I thought you would at least want to wait until the divorce is final....."

She grimaces again. I realize I'm hurting her by talking about things she doesn't want to talk about.

She blows my mind a second time by completely brushing that off. "I thought I did, but I realized today that I really don't want to go back to that house. It's....it's a mausoleum."

"It isn't!" I insist. "Of course you wanted to hold onto memories of your husband."

"I held onto them too tightly. I don't want you to think I'm using a relationship with you to get over him. I don't want you to think a relationship with you is a temporary stopping-over place on the way to somewhere else."

"I don't think that—unless it's you who thinks I'm using you to get over Skyla. I thought you would be worried about me using you as a rebound. If you want to move in with me.....I would be thrilled if you wanted to do that. I would be over the moon. Please... move in with me. I was just waiting for the right time to ask—though I admit I didn't know when the right time to ask was."

She bursts into a grin. "Great. Thank you."

"Thank *you.*" I take a chance and kiss her hands. "I'm thrilled."

She blushes at me. "Me, too. It's gonna be great."

I can't keep away from her. I can't even remember why I felt so rotten just a few minutes ago.

I lean across the table and kiss her. I'd like to grab her right now. I would really like to drag her home with me right now—and we definitely wouldn't be getting any sleep.

Just then, our server comes over and hands me a folded piece of paper. "This is for you, Mr. Hayes."

I look up. "What is it?"

"I don't know, Sir. Those gentlemen over there asked me to give this to you."

The server points across the restaurant. My mind goes dark when I see Lane Prince, Jackson Metcalf, and Niko Holloway sitting together at a booth in the corner.

They all look across the restaurant at me and Piper. All three of those guys must have seen me kissing her.

I attack the paper, unfold it, and read, *Come over here. We need to talk to you.*

I look up and Jackson waves me toward their table.

"What's going on?" Piper asks.

"I'm not sure. They want me to go over there so they can talk to me. They're friends of mine...."

"I know who they are. You better go talk to them." I look up and her eyes soften. "I'll wait for you. Go on."

I leave the paper on the table and cross to sit down next to Lane. "This better be something important—and don't any of you give me any static about going out with Piper. She's great."

"No one is going to give you any static about her," Jackson tells me. "You have good taste. We're all happy for you."

"What is this about, then?" I hear myself snapping at them. I shouldn't.

"Niko has something he wants to say to you," Lane tells me.

I glance at Niko. He's a young guy, but he sure knows how to take care of business. He's as solid as they come and he works his tail off. He runs circles around guys three times his age.

He levels me with a hard stare. I almost feel intimidated by him when he looks at me like that.

"What's up, man?" I ask.

He purses his lips once, shoots a glance past me toward Piper sitting alone at our table, and then turns back to me. "I was driving down Long Island last night—about one-thirty in the morning. I was taking my new Carrera for a spin....and I just happened to be driving through your neighborhood."

The hair on the back of my neck stands on end. I'm not hearing this.

"I spotted your ex sitting in the passenger seat of a van about five blocks from your house," he goes on. "I came up on the van just as she was getting out the passenger door. She ran across the street right in front of my car and dove into the bushes on your side of the road."

I have to swallow to get my voice working. "Are you absolutely certain it was her?"

"Oh, it was her. I had to slow down....because I was driving a little too fast—you know. She looked right at me in the headlights. It was h er."

I look away and spot Piper across the room. She's watching us, but she can't hear our conversation.

"I was gonna tell you the next time I saw you—just to let you know she was snooping around your place," Niko tells me. "Then I just heard about your limo crashing a few hours ago....and I didn't really know who to tell. I mean, the two things could be totally disconnected, right?"

I run my hand across my eyes. "They aren't. Someone cut my brake lines."

Niko stiffens and then glances at Jackson and Lane. "No shit? That's off the chain."

I pull out my wallet and rummage around until I find Detective Beckett's card. "This is the cop who's investigating the incident. I would appreciate it if you could call him and tell him everything. He's the one who's handling this."

Niko dips his chin once. Then he takes out his phone and starts entering Detective Beckett's information into his note-taking app. "No problem. Consider it done."

I glance at the other two men. I want to thank them, but the gratitude tightening my chest is too big even for that.

I hold out my hand to Niko and he takes it. "I owe you for this," I murmur. "I owe all of you big time."

Jackson nods back toward Piper. "Get out of here, man. Go enjoy yourself. You deserve it."

I slip out of their booth and go back to the table where Piper sits waiting for me. "What was that about?" she asks.

"Niko Holloway saw Skyla in my neighborhood last night. She was lurking around at one-thirty in the morning in a van and hiding in the bushes. He's going to report it to Detective Beckett."

Her eyes widen. "Holy crap. I didn't mean this when I said something might turn up."

"If the Police can show that she tampered with the car, she'll get sent away for vehicular homicide. She'll be off the streets. We won't have to deal with her again."

Chapter 29: Piper

I lean across the limo seat to kiss Judah and I immediately get sucked into those lips. I can't pull away.

His hand slips around my waist and he pulls me in a little deeper before he floats off and looks up into my eyes. "Are you sure you don't want me to come with you?"

"You need to get to the office. You've been gone too much as it is." I lean back. "I'll be fine. I just need to get it done."

"Let me know if I can help at all."

"You are." I don't want to stop kissing him. "You're already helping me a lot—more than I could ask for."

The driver opens the limo door for me to get out. I give Judah one more kiss and climb up onto the sidewalk. "I'll call you later!" I tell him through the door.

"Have a good day!" he calls back

The driver shuts the door. I wave at the tinted windows even though I can't see Judah anymore.

The car pulls out of sight and I turn to my house—my old house. I want to get this house cleaned out so I can sell it and never come back here. I've been living here for too long as it is.

I go inside and put my purse on the hall table. Just for a minute, I stand in the hall and take a good look around.

Memories overflow every room in this house—and they're all memories of my dead husband.

Only the memories of the night I spent with Judah interrupt that endless parade of long-forgotten images and pictures from a life that doesn't exist anymore.

I let all those memories wash over me—for the last time. I'm here to pack up my stuff, put my husband's pictures in storage, and start my new life with Judah. I don't want to live in a tomb anymore.

I go into the living room first. I walk past the shelf over the fireplace and look extra closely at each picture one after the other.

My late husband looks as young, as healthy, and as strong and kind and caring in these pictures as he was in life. His brown hair falls over his soft green eyes. The square cut of his jaw and cheeks looks so familiar—like he's right here in front of me right now.

The strange thing is that I hardly ever look at these pictures anymore. I can't remember the last time I stood here and really looked at them—at him.

Those pictures were always just there—like the curtains. I didn't look at them. I didn't think about them. I didn't think about him.

He was just there, too—like the curtains—the curtains in my mind. He was just there to block my view of the outside world and whatever I might possibly find or see out there.

I remember how I used to feel about him. I remember so clearly how much I loved him and how much it hurt to lose him. I remember feeling like I would never live again—never love again.

All those feelings seem so far in the past now. The way I feel about Judah is so much more real.

Judah is my present and my future. There's no place anymore for the past in that present or that future. It's time to put it away for good.

I want to. I'm ready. I'm beyond ready. I cringe when I think how long I've put off the inevitable.

I open a cardboard packing box on the living room coffee table and start stacking the pictures inside. There sure are a lot of them. It's almost like I was trying to cover up the fact that he really wasn't here.

I don't remember having this many pictures of him around the house when he was alive. That would have been creepy.

I fill one box and start on the second one. I empty all the pictures out of the living room.

I take a second box up to the bedroom, put the box on the bed, and start collecting the pictures off of my dresser. There are way too many of them here, too. Man, I really had a problem.

I pile all the pictures on top of each other in a stack so I won't have to go back and forth. I make a big tower and turn toward the bed to take the pictures to the box.

I freeze and my blood runs cold when Skyla steps out of my walk-in closet across the room. Her hair hangs limp and her makeup has smeared down her face like maybe she's been walking outside in the weather.

That makes sense if she's been running around in the Long Island bushes at one-thirty in the morning and hiding from the Police ever since.

She glares at me in a psychotic, mindless trance. My eyes dip to her hand. She's holding a baseball bat.

"I told you to stay away from him!" Her voice quakes and her body trembles. "I told you to keep your hands off my husband!"

I try to keep my voice calm, but I can't do anything with all these pictures in my hands. I really need to find some weapon to defend myself.

"I didn't do anything, Skyla," I quaver. "You and Judah broke up long before....."

"I saw you in our house!" she shrieks. "I saw you in our bed! You stole him from me! You bitch! I'll kill you!"

I try one more time to say, "You cheated on him....." but she doesn't listen.

She lunges for me and raises her bat before I can react. I drop all the pictures on the floor and try to dive out of her way, but she charges too fast.

I stumble and she swings the bat at me. I make one last desperate effort to roll away from that blow.

It cracks me across the back and knocks me flat on the floor. I roar in pain, but I don't have time to think about that before she comes after me again.

She stalks me down and swings right down on top of me. The bat would cave in my head, but I raise my arm instead and the bat smashes down on the bone right below my elbow.

I scream again, but she's already winding up for another swing. I have to get away from her. She really does plan to kill me.

I can't see anything I might be able to use as a weapon. Shards of broken glass from all the broken picture frames cover the floor, but Skyla stands between me and then. I can't get to them fast enough.

She strides toward me raising her bat above her head. I can't use any part of my body to defend myself. I already feel how injured I am. I'll be lucky to get out of this house alive.

My phone is downstairs in my purse on the hall table where I left it. I have to get to it. I have to call someone to help me.

My mind immediately snaps to Judah, but he can't help me now. I'm all alone.

I don't even know if I can stand. That blow to my back broke bones. I don't want to think about how bad my injuries are.

That doesn't matter. I just have to get away from Skyla. She really is going psycho on me.

I kick out at the only thing available to help me. I hook my foot into the chair in front of the dresser, kick it over in front of her feet, and she stumbles.

I blast upright and take off running down the stairs. Adrenaline masks the pain in my back and arm. The pain actually gives me the energy to get down there faster.

I pound down the stairs and hear her cursing at me from the bedroom. I snatch my purse off the table and tear the front door off its hinges on my way outside. I keep on running all the way down the block before I dare to stop.

A bunch of people turn around to stare at me, but I can't relax. I fumble to get my phone out of my purse and call 911.

Chapter 30:
Judah

I storm into the hospital Emergency Department ready to destroy anyone who gets in my way. I barely remember being in here as a patient just yesterday.

I barge up to the nurse's desk and snarl through gritted teeth. "Excuse me. I'm looking for Piper Lagrange."

The nurse behind the desk points past me. "Through those doors, third cubicle on the left."

I blast through the doors and stalk down the ward searching every bed. She better not be hurt. I swear I'll kill someone if she is.

I walk into a curtained cubicle with Detective Beckett and another plain-clothes detective standing on one side. Two doctors in lab coats face a lightbox on the wall.

One of them points to an X-ray with his pen while they discuss something in another language I don't understand.

My blood starts to boil when I see Piper lying on the bed with her arm in a cast. She's wearing a hospital gown. She looks small, weak, and fragile like this.

The doctors and the detectives all turn around when I show up. Piper's eyes snap to my face and she immediately screws up her features in a mask of miserable agony. She starts crying in silent, choking sobs.

I don't wait around to hear what any of the doctors or detectives say. I shove past them to her bed and put my arms around the only parts of her I can reach—her head and upper shoulders.

She completely breaks down as soon as I get there. She clings to me with her good arm, buries her face in my chest, and shakes with aching sobs.

I hug her close, kiss her hair, and murmur in as low a voice as I can, "Shhh. Shhh. It's all right. I'm here."

I become painfully aware of the doctors and both detectives watching us, but I really don't care.

I make a calculated decision to ask Detective Beckett all the questions boiling out of me right now. "What the hell happened?"

"Your ex broke into Ms. Lagrange's house, hid on the premises, and attacked her with a baseball bat," Detective Beckett replies. "She has three rib fractures in her back and a broken arm."

"Your next words better be that you have the psycho bitch in custody," I snarl.

"We have a warrant out for her arrest and we have officers canvasing all her usual known locations. She can't stay hidden for long."

"She killed Carl," I spit. "She tried to kill me. She tampered with my car."

He only nods. "I know. I got Mr. Holloway's statement yesterday. The warrant is for one count of first-degree murder and two counts of attempted murder. She won't get away with this. I promise you that."

I snort. I don't want to believe that, but Piper distracts me by sitting up. She still sniffling and wiping her nose and face on the sleeve of her gown.

I bend over and get in her face. I can't stop touching her hair and face and shoulders. I want to touch more, but I don't want to hurt her.

"Are you okay?" I breathe. "Oh, my God! I wish I had been there! You got away from her! You did great! You're safe now. I'm gonna take you home. You can rest there."

She nods, but I already see her winding up to burst into tears again. This is the last thing she needs.

She was going to move out of that house—the house where her husband died.

This whole thing with Skyla must be the worst déjà vu in history. It's the same nightmare all over again.

It's lucky for everyone that I wasn't there or no one would be trying to arrest Skyla now. She better not try anything with Piper while I'm around. I don't know what I'll do if Skyla does try something.

"Ms. Lagrange will need plenty of rest and painkillers until her ribs heal," one of the doctors tells me. "She won't be able to do anything physically strenuous for at least six to eight weeks. The more active she is, the longer her ribs will take to heal."

I only nod. "That's okay. She can stay home."

"I would advise you to take security precautions until we take your ex-wife into custody," Detective Beckett tells me. "She's obviously much more dangerous than any of us realized. She could try anything, now that she doesn't think she has anything to lose."

"I'll handle it," I mutter. "I have my own security."

Detective Beckett turns to leave. "We'll be in touch as soon as we know anything. I'll call you the minute we take your ex-wife into custody."

I don't answer. Maybe it's better if they don't take Skyla into custody today. Then I'll know where she is. That might not be such a good thing if she keeps pulling shit like this.

If Skyla is half as smart as she thinks she is, she'll be halfway to Siberia by now. She doesn't want to find herself on the same continent as me when I catch up with her.

The two detectives and the two doctors turn away to leave. I turn back to Piper. I want to be alone with her. I want to comfort her at least until she feels better about this.

I sure as hell hope she doesn't change her mind about us because of this. I hope this doesn't send her crawling back into her safe little cocoon of solitude.

I put the doctors and the detectives out of my mind. Silence falls except for Piper's barely audible sobs. I put my arms around her.

"I never did anything to her!" she wails. "I never came between you two or stole you from her or anything! She knows I didn't!"

I hug her head to my chest and let my lips fall on her hair. I can't even answer. Piper never did anything to deserve someone saying those things about her.

I sit on the edge of the bed holding Piper until the nurses come to release her. They give us both another lecture about Piper not doing anything strenuous until her ribs heal.

I buy her a big, fluffy bathrobe from a department store downtown and wrap it around her so she can take her hospital gown off.

The nurses get her into a wheelchair and wheel her out to the curb so she can get into the car. I arrange to take her in a regular passenger car so she can get in and out more easily.

I drive her myself and hold the wheelchair for her to ease herself into it. Then I wheel her to a guest room on the ground floor where she pivots over to the bed.

She groans and hisses and winces a lot every time she moves. She finally settles herself down on the pillows and heaves a sigh before she looks up at me. She really does look miserable.

"This isn't what I had in mind when I asked if I could move in with you," she mumbles.

I sit down next to her and kiss her. "This is exactly what I had in mind when you asked me if you could move in with me."

She snorts and winces again. "Getting attacked by your psycho ex-wife?"

"No, taking care of you no matter what you need."

She tries to control her lips, but emotion gets the better of her. "I'm no good to you like this."

"Hey!" I whisper and cup her cheek to turn her face toward me. "You're even better like this." I take the plunge and say the words that have been on my lips all this time. "I love you. I want you in my life and in my bed. I don't care what condition you're in."

Tears overflow her eyes. "But I want to—and now I can't! It isn't fair—and now I have to wait eight weeks!"

I find myself smiling at her, but the anguish in those eyes brings a lump into my throat. "Maybe we can do a few things—nothing strenuous—a few licks here and there—nothing you can't handle."

She laughs and tears streak down her cheeks at the same time.

"You need to rest and recover," I tell her. "You need to rest and recover from the attack as much as you need to rest and recover from these injuries. You'll heal. It's your precious heart I worry about. I want you to feel safe. You don't need to worry about me. I'll still be here when you get better. Don't worry...and I'll still want you just as m uch."

I kiss her one more time and pull away. I don't need to kiss her or hug her or even do it with her—not as much as I need this.

I need to be here for her and support her and take care of her. I don't care about anything else.

She grabs my hand to hold me back. "Judah......"

I sink back onto the bed next to her. "What is it, baby? What do you need?"

Tears well up in her eyes again. "I....I love you. I just want....I want us to be together....like that....like you said.....like everything you said."

Sheer sunshine happiness floods my heart at those words. I hug her head—the only part of her I can still hug, but that's enough.

I kiss her hair. "I want that, too, baby. Now rest. Don't move or think about anything."

"Would you mind....?" Her eyes dart toward the door. "Would you mind bringing me my phone?"

I burst out laughing. You can't keep this woman down. She'll keep working until someone puts her in her grave. "Sure. I'll get it for you. Stay here."

I get her phone out of the bag of personal effects I brought home from the hospital. She settles back on the pillows tapping the screen with one hand.

I smile at her before I walk out of the room. She'll keep working and running her cases and clients. She won't let this keep her down.

She'll keep running my case, too. She won't let the grass grow under her feet. She wasn't made that way.

I check to make sure we have enough groceries in the fridge for me to make her dinner tonight. I could order something, but I want to cook for her. I want to wait on her hand and foot, but I have something more important to do first.

I walk out of the house. The minute I get into the driveway, cold determination takes over. All the good feelings I shared with her in that room evaporate. I'm back to wanting to kill someone.

I go out to the gate where I find Charlie, my head of security.

"How's Ms. Lagrange, Sir?" he asks me.

"She isn't doing very good, Charlie, to be honest. I want you to double the security around the property."

"Yes, Sir," he clips. "I expected something like that."

"And I want them to be top-of-the-line security—not these rent-a-cops—and they should be armed—heavily armed."

He only dips his chin once. "Yes, Sir. No problem."

"I want you to patrol the grounds around the clock. Skyla made it onto the property once already and now Carl is dead. I don't want to take any chances that she could get onto the property again."

He nods. "Yes, Sir. I'll take care of it."

"And post an armed guard inside the house. Don't put them anywhere they might disturb Piper, but keep the house under guard at all times. Understand? I want them to patrol the house, even the parts we aren't using. Make sure Skyla couldn't be hiding anywhere in unused closets or rooms."

"Of course, Sir. Leave it to me."

I clap him on the shoulder. "Thank you, man. There's a killer on the loose. I don't want to take any chances."

Chapter 31: Piper

J udah opens the front door for me and I step outside for the first time. It's been a month since Skyla attacked me with a baseball bat. My ribs are healing slowly. They still feel sore if I move wrong or press on them, but at least I can walk now.

I step outside and inhale a deep breath of the crisp autumn air. The grounds around the estate smell of rotten leaves and damp soil. Winter is coming.

It feels good to go outside after lying flat on my back for a month, but the line of black Range Rovers in front of me tells me loud and clear that I'm not here to enjoy myself.

The rows of armed security guards around the estate's perimeter also drive home the point that I'm not safe even here. Skyla is still out there.

She hasn't come near the estate again—not with all these armed mercenaries standing guard

She hasn't gotten arrested yet, either. The Police haven't been able to find her even though they've searched everywhere.

Charlie, our head of security, stands next to the center Range Rover holding the door open for me. All I have to do is walk over there and get in.

Getting into and out of these high vehicles will be easier than getting into and out of a limo—not that I've tried it. I can imagine, though. All that bending over would kill me.

Judah escorts me to the car and hovers over me while I get in. He's been unbelievably supportive and caring while I've been laid up with broken ribs and a broken arm.

He cooks meals for me, brings me anything I need, and he doesn't seem to care at all that we haven't been able to have sex since I got hurt. He never even mentions it, but I've been going crazy.

If I drop a hint, he only smiles and reminds me of the doctors' orders not to strain myself. Little does he know I'm straining myself without it.

Sleeping in the same bed next to him drives me out of my mind. I want to touch him and rub my body all over him, but he's too self-possessed even for that.

He keeps telling me he wants to take me completely and he can't do that until I heal. Great. Sometimes I wish he wasn't so caring.

That isn't true. It's touching that he cares so much even about this.

He also shows his caring side by checking every detail of our security around the clock. Security guards even patrol inside the house. They come into the bedroom twice a day to search the closets, bathroom, and even under the bed.

Charlie always apologizes to me for the intrusion, but it actually makes me feel better. I don't have to worry about Skyla leaping out of the shadows to attack me again.

Judah gets into the rear passenger seat next to me. Half the security guys load up in the other three Range Rovers. They check in all directions and keep their weapons with them while the four vehicles pull out of the driveway.

Charlie and three other security guards ride in the same car with me and Judah. All of them constantly glance around everywhere searching for any sign of danger.

The four vehicles rumble down the highway and into Manhattan. This will be the first time I've gone back to my old house since the attack.

Judah and I have decided to clean out the house once and for all. Then we'll put it on the market and get it out of our lives for good. I can't wait.

I just need to get through today. Then I never have to see the house again.

I've already started my new life with Judah. I don't want the old one. I don't want it to intrude on my life at all. I don't even want to think about it.

My pulse starts racing when we get to my old neighborhood. The Range Rovers park in front of the house and all the security guys unload.

They spread through the streets, pour into the house, and come back out. "We searched the house, Mr. Hayes," Charlie tells Judah. "It's all clear. You can go in. The movers are already here."

"Thank you, Charlie," Judah replies and gets out to open my door.

Climbing the front steps used to be so easy. Now it's a hike. I get inside and pause in the entrance hall to catch my breath

The movers are already working all over the house to pack up my old stuff. The furniture, kitchen goods, artwork, and furnishings will go to an estate sale right away. I don't want any of it.

I only care about my personal items. I'm going to keep the pictures of my dead husband, but they'll go into storage where I don't have to deal with them.

Judah touches my arm. "Take a seat. We'll ask you about anything we think you might want to keep."

I nod. We've already discussed this a million times. Nothing that happens here will be a surprise.

I ease myself down on the living room couch. This couch reminds me of Judah. We did it for the first time on this couch. That's one good memory I'll take with me.

The box of pictures still stands on the coffee table where I left it. No one has touched it since I ran out of the house to get away from Skyla.

Judah goes through the house room by room giving instructions to the movers. He even goes upstairs and I hear someone sweeping broken glass off the bedroom floor. Then the glass falls into a trash can.

Charlie and the security team go through the house room by room, too. They keep a sharp eye on the movers, but none of them is Skyla. She isn't here.

Maybe she really did leave the area. Maybe she went on the run from the arrest warrant for Carl's death and two counts of attempted murder. She'd have to be insane to stay in New York with that hanging over her head.

She is insane. I know that now. She's as insane as the girl who killed my husband.

Skyla is completely out of her mind. She's living in a fantasy world where she and Judah are still together even though she's a prostitute in the back room of a Bronx strip club.

I pull the box of pictures toward me. I have nothing else to do until someone comes to ask me something.

Judah already knows what I want to do with everything in this house. He can tell the movers as well as I can. I'm only here to make an appearance—to appease the ghosts that still live in this house.

Will they keep living here after I move out and sell it? What happens to ghosts when the people they haunt move on?

I lift out a picture of my dead husband. I can't even think of him as that anymore. He isn't my husband anymore. He's no more my husband than Judah is Skyla's husband. That relationship ended a long time ago.

It didn't end in my mind, though. It only ended when Judah and I got together. Right up until then, I still thought I was married. Maybe I'm the crazy one living in a fantasy world. In fact, I know I am.

I lean forward to put the picture back in the box and take out another one. God only knows why I'm taking out another one. I know what my dead ex-husband looked like. I carry around his face etched into my brain.

I look up at the box.....and freeze to my seat when a board in the living room floor levers out of position. I sit there slack-jawed in stunned disbelief as it flips into the room, bangs down on the hardwood floor, and then another one pivots out of place.

I'm not sure what I'm seeing until Skyla sits up and then climbs out of the hole. I'm so surprised that I don't react—not until she pulls a shotgun out of the hollow with her.

"JUDAH!!" I bellow. "JUDAH—SHE'S HERE!! SKYLA'S HERE!! JUDAH—COME HERE!!"

I hear footsteps pounding all over the house, but they can't get here fast enough. Skyla straightens up in front of me.

She hardens her features into the same mask of deadly fury as her last attack. She raises the shotgun and aims it at me.

I dive for cover just as the gun goes off. I might hurt myself, but I'd rather spend the next two months in bed than get my head blown off.

The shot smashes into the back of the couch—right where I was just sitting.

I throw myself onto the cushion first in some hopeless effort not to hurt myself, but I'm still too exposed here.

I roll off onto the floor as she unloads a second time. The blast shatters the glass coffee table and broken glass rains all over me.

I scream and roar at the same time. She stalks across the room getting closer.

I scramble into reverse and scoot behind the couch, but she rotates around the wrecked coffee table pounding gunshots at me from all directions—or it seems that way.

Those shots blast into the floorboards, the side table, the walls, and the end of the couch. Stuffing, splintered wood, and shattered metal fly in my face.

I can't even take one arm off the floor to protect myself. I still have one arm in a sling. I have to use the other one to crawl.

Nowhere is safe from her. Where is everyone? Why aren't the security guys coming to my rescue?

I can't see anything with her gun smashing the living room to pieces all around me. I dive around the other side of the couch, but she only follows me. Now I have nowhere left to hide.

She comes after me and I hear men yelling in the distance. I can't make out the words or even tell where they're coming from.

More gunshots go off out of sight and Skyla wheels in that direction. She unloads to one side and a bunch of the security guys have to dive for cover. I can't tell if she hits any of them.

She starts to swing her gun around to aim at me again. How many shots does she have left?

Out of nowhere, Judah dives across the room and tackles her onto the floor. They both go flying, slam down hard on the floorboards, and her gun sails out of her grasp.

It skids across the floor away from me. I'm not strong enough to get up and go after it.

Judah and Skyla go after it, though. They both rocket to their feet and lunge for the weapon at the same time.

They get there at the same time and they both grab it. They wrestle over it for a split second before Judah rips it out of her hands and kicks her away.

She cartwheels across the room, vaults to her feet, and lets out a feral bellow before she dives for him again.

In a lightning move of pure instinct, he rotates onto his back, brings the gun up, and fires straight into her chest. At the same instant, the security guys unload on her from behind and riddle her with bullets.

I can't watch. I huddle under my arms and clamp my hands over my ears to block out the noise.

When the shooting stops and I dare to look up, Skyla lies sprawled on the floor in a pool of blood.

Judah lies on the floor, too. He lies on his back with his head up and the gun still aimed at the spot where Skyla was just standing. It's over. She's dead.

Chapter 32: Piper

A female paramedic with a brown ponytail presses her flat fingertips against my lower back. "How about here? Do you have any pain down here?"

"No," I mutter. "I don't have any more pain than I did before the shooting. I didn't get hurt. I'm fine."

"Then I guess you just have to go home—and try not to hurt yourself again."

"I wasn't trying to hurt myself this time."

She gives me a look and goes back to her waiting ambulance. She and the other paramedics have enough to deal with transporting the injured security guards to the hospital.

Charlie is one of them. He got hit in the shoulder by one of Skyla's shotgun blasts. Two other guards suffered serious injuries and five got hit by stray buckshot.

I shouldn't give the paramedics attitude, but I just want to get out of here, especially when the Medical Examiner's team comes out with Skyla in a body bag.

I can't even be grateful that she's finally dead. She'll never bother us again, but why did it have to happen like this?

As soon as the paramedic leaves, Detective Beckett comes over to me. He's been biding his time while she checks me out.

He's been using the time to interview Judah, Charlie, and all the other security guards about what happened. Now it's my turn.

Fortunately, Judah comes with him, but Judah doesn't sit down next to me or put his arms around me or anything like that. He stays standing and facing me next to Detective Beckett.

Detective Beckett stops in front of me. "Are you ready to give a statement, Ms. Lagrange?"

I nod at nothing.

"So what happened first?"

"I was sitting in the living room looking at some old family photographs and she came out from under the living room floorboards. She must have loosened them. She pushed out two of them and then she climbed out and started shooting at me."

He only nods. Of course he already knows. He and the rest of the cops already searched the house from top to bottom.

They've already seen the loose floorboards lying out of place and the hole under the floor where Skyla climbed out of her hiding place. I'm not telling Detective Beckett anything he doesn't already know.

"Then what happened?" he asks.

"I called out for Judah....but he didn't come quick enough, so I had to dive onto the floor to get away from her gunshots. She followed me around the couch and then all the guys showed up."

He nods again. They know all that, too. Of course the security guys already told the Police everything.

There are too many witnesses and Skyla was already wanted for killing one man and trying to kill two other people including me. This case probably won't even go to an inquiry.

Detective Beckett only says, "We'll be closing this case now, but we'll need you and Mr. Hayes to make yourselves available for any further questioning if we need to clarify anything. Are you both cool with that?"

I nod and Judah says, "Of course." This must be the shortest Police interview in the history of the human race. This case is so open and shut that it never really opened in the first place.

Detective Beckett says, "You can take her home," to Judah and walks away.

Judah stands there staring down at me for a minute before he sits next to me on the Range Rover's rear bumper.

"Are you okay?" he murmurs. "Like—really?"

"Yeah, I'm okay," I murmur back. "I just want to get the hell out of here. I don't care if you throw away everything in the house. I don't ever want to see this place again."

"All right. Get in the car and I'll take you home."

He helps me stand up, opens the front passenger door for me, and stands over me while I get into the seat.

He shuts the door, goes back inside the house, and comes out with two cardboard boxes. He puts them in the back. I don't have to wonder what's in them.

He gets behind the wheel and we drive back to his house in silence. I don't know what to say or even what to think. I have to reevaluate my whole world, now that Skyla isn't out there waiting for me.

The security guards take just as many precautions about letting us inside the grounds. They either haven't heard the news or Charlie and Judah haven't given the guards orders to change anything.

It's going to take me and Judah a while to let down our defenses—if we ever do. I don't want the security guards to go away. I don't want them to slacken their vigilance. Something else might happen.

I've started feeling safe in this house thanks to them. I don't want to give that up—not yet.

Judah opens the door for me to enter the house—our house. This is my home now. I'll never go back to that brownstone on 73rd Street.

I go straight to the bedroom on the ground floor. This is our bedroom now—at least until it gets easier for me to climb stairs.

I kick off my shoes, take my phone out of my purse, and put it on the nightstand within arm's reach. That way, I can work without getting out of bed.

Judah comes over to me and takes my one good hand in his. His eyes light up for the first time since we left Manhattan. "Do we need to start sending you around the town with a gun belt around your hips from now on?"

"Stop it. You were the one who shot her, not me."

He laughs. He actually looks happy again. "I think you deserve a reward for foiling the culprit."

I snort at him. "Culprit? What are you—a lawyer?"

He won't stop beaming at me. "I'm just trying to lighten the mood."

"I think you lightened it enough already."

He laughs again and leans in to kiss me. He kisses me lightly—like he wants to be gentle with me.

That kiss keeps going and getting stronger. He hasn't kissed me like this since before I got hurt.

He starts to put his arm behind my back and stops himself in time. He pulls away grinning. "Nice try, but no dice."

"You were the one who started this. I was just standing here minding my own business before you came along."

"What do you think of my suggestion?"

"What suggestion? I didn't hear anything."

"I suggested giving you a reward for catching the culprit." He laughs at his own joke.

"Why am I getting rewarded? I didn't do anything. You're the one who deserves a reward."

His cheeks color. "All right. If you insist."

I raise my eyebrows. "Really? Are you sure you can handle that kind of stimulation?"

"I'm sure I can, but that isn't what I had in mind."

"What reward would you like? Name your price."

He explodes in laughter again. His eyes shine in ways I haven't seen in over a month. He never lets himself look at me this way.

He sure is looking at me this way now. He allows his hungry eyes to roam down my body and back up to my face and hair and lips and neck.

"So....is this a reward for me or a reward for you?" he asks.

"You tell me. I don't even know what you're going to do."

"Promise me you won't do anything that might hurt you."

"Okay. I promise."

He compresses his lips to hold back another blushing smirk. He walks around behind me and starts unbuckling the strap on my arm sling.

He takes it off very gently and then slowly, deliberately, painstakingly starts to undress me.

The look in his eyes makes me shiver, but I can't even do anything. I just have to stand here and let him peel off my clothes one excruciating piece at a time.

He eases my jacket off my good arm and then maneuvers it over my cast. He holds my eyes spellbound while he slowly, carefully unbuttons my blouse one aching button at a time.

My skin tingles when he slides my blouse off. I tremble before him in my bra when he goes down on one knee, unbuttons my pants, and drags them and my panties down my trembling thighs.

I'm already saturated to the limit by the time he pulls them over my feet and pushes them aside. He doesn't get up.

He cups my ass in both hands and nuzzles his nose and tongue between my legs. His hot, slippery mouth finds my most sensitive tissues and teases me to ragged ecstasy.

I have to be careful not to pant too hard or I'll hurt my ribs. I can't really move. I just have to stand here and let these epic waves of bliss wash over me.

This is the first time he's touched me since I got hurt. My desire explodes off the charts, but I have to keep still and take it. I can't make any sudden moves or gyrate on his face or buck in the throes of passion.

Of course he knows exactly what he's doing to me. His hot breath sears my swollen slit and my juices ooze into his ravenous mouth.

He stands up way too soon, but his eyes tell me he isn't anywhere near done. He unclips my bra and slides it down my arms.

"Lie down on the bed and spread your legs for me," he murmurs in an irresistible undertone of command.

I sit down on the bed, lower myself very carefully onto the bedspread, and let my thighs fall apart. That feeling of exposing myself for his pleasure—this is all I've dreamed about for the last month.

He sinks into the bed between my legs and goes back to slowly dragging his masterful tongue through my saturated frills. My breath quickens and my body quivers all over with desire.

I don't know how far he'll go, but he'll take me to the farthest horizon on a dreamy hurricane of rapture. This moment crosses the line. There's no going back.

I'll get better. I'll get stronger. I'll be able to thrash on his brutal thrusts. He'll be able to hold me down and bend me over and crush me against the wall again.

I'll be able to scream in agony when he makes me climax again and again and again. I'll be able to pleasure him and hear those low growls and groans of his primal delight when I take him to the stars.

Right now, I can just swim in this sea of tranquil bliss and feel his hands touching me, his mouth devouring me, and all the love in both our hearts coming together in perfection all our own. It doesn't get any better than this.

<u>End of Book 2.</u>

Keep Reading

The Billionaires' Club Series: Book 3: Enemy Betrothed

Niko Holloway is the youngest member of the Billionaires' Club, but no one can deny that he's one of the biggest cutthroats on the block. He's ruthless, determined, and wins the respect of everyone, including billionaires many decades older and more experienced.

Not everyone in the club admires Niko, though. When the deal of a lifetime requires him to partner with his worst enemy, Niko instantly smells a rat and all his spider senses snap to high alert for any sign that his old nemesis will try to ruin him for the second time.

Melody Gottlieb has better things to do than get involved in her father's business. She's horrified when she learns that her father and brother have made her a condition of a business deal with their worst enemy—the man who supposedly screwed her father over the last time.

The whole world could explode when Niko and Melody meet at the altar with both of them planning to destroy the other before their enemies destroy them first.

You can find it at your favorite book retailer.

Get All of AE Moran's Free Books

S ign Up Once—Get all A.E. Moran's free books including brand new releases

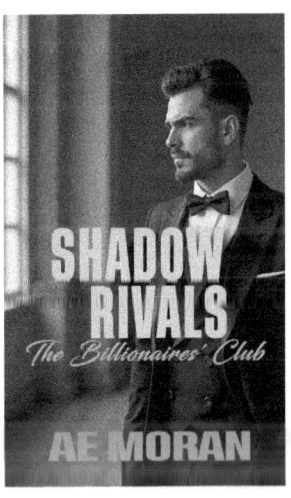

Holden Seager is hot, magnetic, and filthy, stinking, obscenely rich. He commands a room the minute he walks in the door. So what happens when meets another shark as powerful, as charismatic, and as successful as he is—not to mention ten years younger? When these two meet across the negotiating table, one of them will walk away the undisputed winner. The other will walk away with nothing.

Or so it seems.

Unless they're best friends.

When the business deal of a lifetime falls flat on its face and neither of these titans knows how to bring it back to life, this might be the opportunity Dayna Turner has been waiting for.

There's just one problem. She works as an assistant to one of these powerful men....and she's in love with the other. It's a recipe for disaster and heartbreak—unless Dayna can pull off an even bigger coup that will leave them all richer, happier, and more closely connected than ever. The alternative is the destruction of everything all three of them have worked so hard to build.

Sign up at www.authoraemoran.com to read it for free.

About AE Moran

A.E Moran is the contemporary romance pen name for Theo Mann.

I write 70 books per year—and yes, before you ask, all these books are my original creative work. Nothing written under my name is AI-generated or ghostwritten because I write better than AI and any ghostwriter out there.

People don't read fiction for entertainment or to escape from reality. People read fiction to see their humanity reflected in another person's character and story.

This is my promise to you. When you read my books, you'll see your own humanity reflected in the characters and stories. I take this commitment to my readers very seriously. My books are an intimate form of communication between us. I would never disrespect my readers by turning that over to a machine or another writer. This is my bond between me and you as my reader.

I write 20,000 words per day as my daily work output. If anyone with a public platform would like to challenge me to prove this in a controlled environment, feel free to contact me on this website's contact page.

I worked as a professional ghostwriter for fifteen years. Now I'm going for the Guinness World Record by writing 700 books over the next ten years and 1400 books over the next twenty years, all originally written by me. See my website for the full book list.

I'm also the author of *Proof for the Existence of God* and the *Crimes Against Fiction* blog. You can find all my nonfiction work at www.cr imes-against-fiction.com.

If you have a story idea, or if you would like me to explore a series in more depth, or if you'd like me to explore a character by writing a spinoff series about that character or world, leave me a message on my website's contact page. I answer all reader emails, so ask me anything, tell me what you liked and didn't like, and let me know where you'd like your favorite series to go. I would love to hear your ideas and find out what you'd like to read next.

You can find out more at www.theomann.com or at www.author aemoran.com.

Also by AE Moran (so far)

Standalone Novels

Heart on a Knife Edge

Dream Dimension

Just Friends

Back From the Dead

Damaged

Small Town Reunion

Series

Firehouse Blues (Books 1-10)

Turning Point Ranch (Books 1-10)

The Billionaires' Club (Books 1-10)

Paradise Cruises (Book 1-8)

Royal House (1-10)

Summerton Estates (1-10)

www.ingramcontent.com/pod-product-compliance
Lightning Source LLC
Chambersburg PA
CBHW052030020726
47501CB00004B/1331